LEGO® CITY

DEEP-SEA TREASURE DIVE

By Trey King
Illustrated by Sean Wang
and Greg Hyland

SCHOLASTIC INC.

All rights reserved. Published by Scholastic Inc., *Publishers since 1920.* SCHOLASTIC and associated logos are trademarks and/or registered trademarks of Scholastic Inc.

The publisher does not have any control over and does not assume any responsibility for author or third-party websites or their content.

ISBN 978-0-545-90591-6

10 9 8 7 6 5 4 3 2 1   16 17 18 19 20
                                                                      40
Printed in the U.S.A.
First printing 2016

Designed by Angela Jun

A diver is in his submarine exploring the deep, dark ocean. He is looking for a sunken ship and its treasure. *It sure is spooky down here*, he thinks to himself.

The diver finally finds what he is looking for—the sunken ship.

He needs to be careful! The ship is surrounded by sharks.

But as the diver gets closer, he sees something ghostly nearby that scares him.

"What's that?" he cries.

The diver doesn't plan to stick around and find out.
He returns to the surface and calls for pickup.

Back at the deep-sea vessel, he tells the rest of his team what he saw.

The crew has a good laugh at the ghost story, and no one else is afraid.

"Put on your gear, team," says the captain. "We're going after that treasure."

The submarines are lowered into the water.
Together, the small fleet explores the deep sea.

Their subs are all different sizes. Some only hold one person, and some can hold many.

At the bottom of the ocean, the team finds a coral reef. Schools of brightly colored fish swim by. There is even an octopus hiding.

One diver gets too close to the octopus. The diver is scared. But the octopus is scared of the diver, too! They both swim away fast. The octopus leaves behind a trail of ink to hide his escape.

The team finds the sunken ship again. They don't see a ghost, but they do see a lot of sharks. It is too dangerous to explore while the sharks are nearby.

The captain has a plan to get those sharks out of there. She radios her ship on the surface for help.

"Send down a diver in a shark cage with some bait. That will distract these sharks," she says.

It works! The sharks all swim toward the bait and away from the ship.

The diver spots part of the treasure—a gigantic gem. But he also sees the ghost! It's holding the gem.

The diver wants that gem. But before he can reach for it, the ghost darts away with the gem.

While the diver chases the ghost, his crewmates look for the rest of the treasure near the ship.

First, they use their lights to brighten up the dark ocean floor.

Second, they use their subs and scooters to clear away the seaweed and sand.

Finally, they use the sub's arms to pick up rocks. That's when they find the lost treasure chest!

Meanwhile, the diver sees something in a nearby cave. He's scared, but it could be the ghost with that giant gem!

The diver shines his light inside the cave and sees the sparkling gem! It's in the tentacles of a rare white octopus. It wasn't a ghost after all!

Just then, the captain radios, "We found the treasure! Head to the surface."

"I guess we all got some treasure today," the diver says as he swims to the surface.

TO

FROM

DATE

DEVOTIONS
for MOMS
(90 DAYS)

Ellen Banks Elwell

Tyndale House Publishers, Inc. Wheaton, Illinois

TYNDALE is a registered trademark of Tyndale House Publishers, Inc.

Tyndale's quill logo is a trademark of Tyndale House Publishers, Inc.

Devotions for Moms (90 Days)

Copyright © 2005 by Ellen Banks Elwell. All rights reserved.

Cover photograph © by Alexandra Grablewski/Getty Images. All rights reserved.

Author photo © 2000 by Lewek Photography. All rights reserved.

Some material previously published in Quiet Moments of Hope for Moms, Quiet Moments of Encouragement for Moms, Quiet Moments of Wisdom for Moms, and Quiet Moments of Faith for Moms, copyright © 1999 by Ellen Banks Elwell. All rights reserved.

Designed by Julie Chen

Unless otherwise indicated, all Scripture quotations are taken from the Holy Bible, New Living Translation, copyright © 1996. Used by permission of Tyndale House Publishers, Inc., Wheaton, Illinois 60189. All rights reserved.

Scripture quotations marked NIV are taken from the Holy Bible, New International Version®. NIV®. Copyright © 1973, 1978, 1984 by International Bible Society. Used by permission of Zondervan Publishing House. All rights reserved.

Scripture quotations marked "NKJV" are taken from the New King James Version. Copyright © 1979, 1980, 1982 by Thomas Nelson, Inc. Used by permission. All rights reserved.

Scripture quotations marked TLB are taken from The Living Bible copyright ©1971. Used by permission of Tyndale House Publishers, Inc., Wheaton, Illinois 60189. All rights reserved.

ISBN 1-4143-0777-2

Printed in the United States of America

10   09   08   06   05
7   6   5   4   3   2   1

WORK

GIVE HER THE REWARD SHE HAS EARNED, AND LET HER
WORKS BRING HER PRAISE AT THE CITY GATE.   *Proverbs 31:31, NIV*

*W*hat might a description for a mom look like if it appeared in a local newspaper?

> *Wanted: A creative and patient woman to be a cook, chaplain, good listener,
> fashion consultant, decorator, recreation expert, teacher, chauffeur, psychologist,
> nurse, artist, gardener, economist, communication advisor, entertainer, purchasing
> agent, lawyer, and accountant. No pay, but excellent benefits!*

Another job description of a mom is found in Proverbs 31, which points out
both character qualities and actions of the mother it portrays. It's impossible for
any of us to live up to the example of this woman (or composite of women), but
the chapter definitely gives us helpful principles to inspire us.

We are encouraged to be

- *Merciful to the poor.* This woman doesn't shrink from helping others.
- *Observant.* Verse 27 informs us that she watches carefully all that goes on
  throughout her household.
- *Trustworthy.* Her family can rely on her character and integrity.
- *Helpful.* She opens her hands to the needy.
- *Energetic.* She plants her own garden; she quilts her own bedspread.
- *Reverent toward God.* She honors, obeys, and spends time with him.
- *Wise.* She gives instructions with kindness.
- *Dignified.* She is worthy of respect because her commitment to God lies at
  the foundation of everything she does.

Wow! This woman is worth so much that it's hard to put a price tag on her.
Don't be intimidated by this woman, moms; be inspired! With God's help, we
can each be a treasure to our family.

> *God,*
> *We sometimes feel overwhelmed with all our responsibilities. We could never*
> *attempt to be an effective mom without your help. May we stay close to you,*
> *finding strength and wisdom to meet each day. Amen.*

HEART

My heart is confident in you, O God; no wonder
I can sing your praises!

Psalm 57:7

*G*od has given us responsibility to choose what we invite into our hearts. We can choose to focus on God and take in messages of beauty, hope, joy, and courage. Or we can choose to take in messages of pessimism and cynicism. Whichever direction we lean will determine the type of heart we grow. Only a heart that trusts in God can praise him and reflect his glory to others.

God is the author of *beauty*. We see it each day, but we don't always notice it. We see it in flowers, snow, colors, the features of our child, or music. We have little opportunities to celebrate the beauty of God's creation each day.

God is the author of *hope*. As the classic hymn reminds me, "My hope is built on nothing less than Jesus' blood and righteousness."

God is the author of *joy*. "The joy of the Lord is your strength" (Nehemiah 8:10).

God is the author of *courage*. Psalm 27:14 (NIV) teaches, "Wait for the Lord; be strong and take heart and wait for the Lord." Courage is surrounded like two bookends by waiting on the Lord.

If we want to have full hearts for our families, we will frequently run to God, who is the source of beauty, hope, joy, and courage.

Father,
Thank you that you are the author of all these qualities of the heart. May you
enlarge our hearts for the roles you have given us. Amen.

OBEDIENCE

YOU KNOW THESE THINGS—NOW DO THEM! THAT IS THE
PATH OF BLESSING.   *John 13:17*

We sometimes hear a mom say, "I feel so blessed!" What might have prompted her to feel that way? A clean bill of health from the doctor? The birth of a long-awaited child? These are wonderful blessings. But we must be careful not to limit our perception of blessings only to things we receive. In John 13 Jesus taught his disciples that obedience brings blessing. Specifically, he taught that blessing comes through humble service to others—hearing God's instructions to serve one another and putting the instructions into action.

Some years ago one of my friends died of cancer, leaving three sons who are friends of my sons. Shortly before she died, I was leaving her house and asked if there was anything more I could do. She said, "Just keep in touch with my boys." I took her request seriously, and great blessing has been mine. Whether it's been giving the boys rides, sending cards, praying for them, taking them out for donuts, giving them pizza parties for their birthdays, or giving them gifts, the joy I have received in doing those things is something I will always carry in my heart.

We are blessed (happy, joyful, fulfilled), not because of what we know, but because of what we do with what we know. We will find our greatest joy in obeying Christ by serving others.[1]

Father,
Thank you for the blessing that obedience brings to our lives. Our own souls
are truly nourished. Amen.

LOVE

MY COMMAND IS THIS: LOVE EACH OTHER AS I HAVE LOVED YOU. GREATER LOVE HAS NO ONE THAN THIS, THAT HE LAY DOWN HIS LIFE FOR HIS FRIENDS. YOU ARE MY FRIENDS IF YOU DO WHAT I COMMAND. I NO LONGER CALL YOU SERVANTS, BECAUSE A SERVANT DOES NOT KNOW HIS MASTER'S BUSINESS. INSTEAD, I HAVE CALLED YOU FRIENDS, FOR EVERYTHING THAT I LEARNED FROM MY FATHER I HAVE MADE KNOWN TO YOU. YOU DID NOT CHOOSE ME, BUT I CHOSE YOU AND APPOINTED YOU TO GO AND BEAR FRUIT—FRUIT THAT WILL LAST. THEN THE FATHER WILL GIVE YOU WHATEVER YOU ASK IN MY NAME. THIS IS MY COMMAND: LOVE EACH OTHER.

John 15:12-17, NIV

How do we understand love, and how do we measure it? With five words: "as I have loved you." Jesus left both a standard and a personal example for us to follow. He doesn't ask us to do anything he hasn't already done.

First, he laid down his life for us (15:13). In order for me to love, I may need to forfeit something valuable to me for the sake of another person. This may involve giving up some of my desires or expectations, or experiencing a greater or lesser degree of inconvenience.

Second, Jesus contrasted servants and friends to teach us that he not only treats us kindly, but he also shares his very thoughts with us (15:15). He has chosen to commune with us and be close to us. This must have been very difficult for him to do with his disciples when he knew that some would doubt him, betray him, deny him, or run away from him. His example inspires us to continue to commune with a husband who disappointed us or a child who disobeyed us.

Third, Jesus took initiative and action with his disciples. He did not sit back and wait for them to come to him, but he reached out to them (15:16). Our families will remember us most for how we cared and reached out to them.

How we follow Christ's example needs to be thought through with integrity and honesty, asking God for his wisdom, strength, and grace. Because when we choose to love, the world sees that we are God's disciples.

Father,
Thank you that you love us perfectly. Please forgive us for the lack of love we sometimes have for others. We need the warmth of your love in hearts that would be cold without you. Amen.

LOVE

FOR SINCE WE WERE RESTORED TO FRIENDSHIP WITH GOD
BY THE DEATH OF HIS SON WHILE WE WERE STILL HIS ENEMIES,
WE WILL CERTAINLY BE DELIVERED FROM ETERNAL PUNISHMENT BY
HIS LIFE. SO NOW WE CAN REJOICE IN OUR WONDERFUL NEW RELATIONSHIP WITH
GOD—ALL BECAUSE OF WHAT OUR LORD JESUS CHRIST HAS DONE FOR US IN
MAKING US FRIENDS OF GOD.

Romans 5:10-11

My five-year-old son, Jordan, and I were walking home from the park hand in hand. He must have been enjoying our time together because he looked up at me and said, "Mommy, you're loveful and beautiful and heartful." "Jordan, would you say that again?" I asked as my heart did a little flip. "You're loveful and beautiful and heartful," he repeated. "Would you tell me that every day for the rest of my life?" I asked, laughing. Although I had never heard of *loveful* or *heartful*, I now think they are some of the most wonderful words in the language—Jordan's five-year-old language. I am still warmed by the memory of his words.

As wonderful as Jordan's words were, I realize that they were spoken on a day when he was five, life was wonderful, and Mom seemed perfect. On rare occasions when he repeats those words today (he's now a young man who knows that life can be difficult and that Mom is not perfect), the words mean even more.

On days when I don't feel particularly loved, secure, or confident, I remember God's *objective* words. According to Romans 5:10-11, the love that prompted Christ to die for me while I was still his enemy is the same love that is available to me today through the presence of God's Spirit in my heart. Those have to be the most loving words I've ever heard.

> Father,
> Thank you for sending your son to die for us. The only way we'll ever begin to love others like you have loved us is by staying close to you. In the name of Jesus, amen.

WITNESS

WE ARE CHRIST'S AMBASSADORS, AND GOD IS USING US TO
SPEAK TO YOU. WE URGE YOU, AS THOUGH CHRIST HIMSELF
WERE HERE PLEADING WITH YOU, "BE RECONCILED TO GOD!"

2 Corinthians 5:20

When I visit Washington DC, I like to drive past embassies of ambassadors from other countries. The architectural designs of the buildings reflect the countries that are represented.

Ambassadors are diplomatic officers of high rank who represent one nation in the capital of another, skillfully acting on behalf of their government. Although bound by instructions and beliefs from their homeland, ambassadors exercise considerable authority with discretion. For ambassadors to be effective, they must act acceptably in the receiving country.

When we enter into a relationship with God, we too become ambassadors with a message. As mothers, we are ambassadors first to our children, and they live in the "embassy" along with us—the embassy of our home. If God's Spirit is present in our lives, they will see whom we represent. The message we have been given is that through Christ we can have a relationship with God. When humans rebelled against God, we became his enemies, but God provided a way for us to be forgiven through Jesus' death on the cross. When we see our need for God, desire a relationship with him, and turn to Christ, he takes away our guilt and gives us his righteousness.

Our responsibility is to represent God as tactfully as we can because we are messengers of peace. Our daily briefing on God's plan for the world comes through the time we spend in his Word. We represent the King of kings, and our homes are embassies. What a privileged position we hold.

God,
Thank you that you have chosen us to represent you. May we do it with accurate information and tact that come from you. Amen.

FAITH

Jesus also said, "Here is another illustration of what the Kingdom of God is like: A farmer planted seeds in a field, and then he went on with his other activities. As the days went by, the seeds sprouted and grew without the farmer's help."

Mark 4:26-27

For any mom who likes to garden, here's an object lesson to try with your young kids. During the fall, take your children to a gardening store and purchase tulip or daffodil bulbs. The pictures on the packages will show what colors the flowers will be.

After you plan which bulbs will go where in your yard, plant them with your children. The kids will be amazed to learn that in five or six months the bulbs will begin to shoot up from the ground, grow, and finally bloom. The activity of planting bulbs will probably raise some questions: Why do we have to wait so long for the flowers to come up? How do we know they will really be red?

The questions children have about planting bulbs are similar to some of the questions we have about our Christian faith. In both situations we learn that we need to follow the instructions and wait for God to work. When we plant bulbs, we trust the instructions on the package, wait for growth, and then enjoy the beauty. The same is true of our faith. We trust the instructions God has given us in the Bible, we choose to obey his guidelines and direction for our lives, and then we wait for the beauty! We also learn that growth doesn't happen immediately—it takes time.

God,
Thank you for your Word, which instructs us how to plant seeds of faith and godliness. Please give us patience as we trust you for growth. Amen.

PRAISE

*E*arly this morning I praised God while I watched a sand crab. I had just completed an early morning walk along the oceanfront where my family is vacationing, and as I was sitting in the sand, I noticed some movement out of the corner of my eye. Looking closer, I discovered a sand crab about four or five inches in diameter with two beady eyes sticking up from the rest of its body. The crab came up out of its hole, pushed some sand out, and then sat there awhile looking at me, eventually going back underground. The routine was repeated several more times until I got up to leave.

As I watched the sand crab, I thought about how many fascinating creatures God has created. Since I am a finite creature, I can only be in one place at a time to enjoy his creation. The creatures I could see this morning included sand crabs, jellyfish, and seagulls. But God is omnipresent, able to be everywhere at once, so he can see all the creatures in the world at the same time!

When I praise God for how wonderful and big he is, my perspective changes. I'm reminded how dependent I am on him, and I'm also reminded that if he is big enough to have created and sustained the sand crab in Gulf Shores, Alabama; the giraffe in Tanzania; and the panda in China, he's big enough to take care of me.

God,
Thank you that you can be everywhere at once, watching over all your
creation, and still care about us and our families. We're encouraged to run to
you anytime, anywhere. Amen.

[A VIRTUOUS WIFE] CAREFULLY WATCHES ALL THAT GOES ON IN HER HOUSEHOLD AND DOES NOT HAVE TO BEAR THE CONSEQUENCES OF LAZINESS.   *Proverbs 31:27*

*W*henever I speak to groups of young moms, I reassure them that I found the early years of motherhood to be the most challenging. I think I felt that way for a couple of reasons. One was that during the years my children were young, I experienced many, many interruptions. Another reason was that when they were little, I didn't seem to have a lot to show for all my efforts at the end of any given day. If you can identify with any of these feelings, you'll enjoy the following story:

> *Too many times women are made to feel that they should apologize for being mothers and housewives. In reality, such roles can be noble callings. When I was on the faculty of the University of Pennsylvania, there were gatherings from time to time to which faculty members brought their spouses. Inevitably, some woman lawyer or sociologist would confront my wife with the question, "And what is it that you do, my dear?" My wife, who is one of the most brilliantly articulate individuals I know, had a great response: "I am socializing two homo-sapiens in the dominant values of the Judeo-Christian tradition in order that they might be instruments for the transformation of the social order into the teleologically prescribed utopia inherent in the eschaton." When she followed that with, "And what is it that you do?" the other person's "a lawyer" just wasn't that overpowering.*[2]

I love that story! We can become so weary of doing the menial tasks that it's easy to lose sight of the great privilege God has given us—to influence and mold young lives for his Kingdom.

> *Lord of life,*
> *Thank you for the gift of children. We are so rich. Please empower us with your love, strength, and wisdom so we will raise children who will help to further your Kingdom. Amen.*

ANIMALS

THE LORD IS MY SHEPHERD; I SHALL NOT WANT. HE MAKES
ME TO LIE DOWN IN GREEN PASTURES; HE LEADS ME BESIDE
THE STILL WATERS. HE RESTORES MY SOUL; HE LEADS ME IN THE
PATHS OF RIGHTEOUSNESS FOR HIS NAME'S SAKE. YEA, THOUGH I WALK THROUGH
THE VALLEY OF THE SHADOW OF DEATH, I WILL FEAR NO EVIL; FOR YOU ARE WITH
ME; YOUR ROD AND YOUR STAFF, THEY COMFORT ME. YOU PREPARE A TABLE
BEFORE ME IN THE PRESENCE OF MY ENEMIES; YOU ANOINT MY HEAD WITH OIL;
MY CUP RUNS OVER. SURELY GOODNESS AND MERCY SHALL FOLLOW ME ALL THE
DAYS OF MY LIFE; AND I WILL DWELL IN THE HOUSE OF THE LORD FOREVER.

Psalm 23, NKJV

One time a little boy was heard misquoting this verse. He said, "The Lord is my shepherd—what more shall I want?" He had the right idea.

The animal most frequently mentioned in the Bible is a sheep. Sheep are basically helpless creatures that depend on their shepherds for food, rest, and protection. Although they are kept in flocks, some sheep have a tendency to wander off and get into trouble. As much as we do not like to admit it, human beings are a lot like sheep. We are stubborn, we tend to follow the crowd, we are fearful, and we sometimes get into things that we shouldn't. Like sheep, we need someone to follow—someone who cares for us and wants to protect us.

It is interesting that the meaning or significance of all seven of the Old Testament names for God is seen in Psalm 23: The Lord will provide. The Lord will heal or restore. The Lord our peace. The Lord our righteousness. The Lord is there. The Lord our banner. The Lord my shepherd.

On days when we feel the strain of our family's financial pressures, we can thank God that he is the Lord who provides. When we feel tension or conflict in a family relationship, we can thank him that he is the Lord our peace. At times when we feel confused and uncertain, we can thank God that he is our shepherd. Not only is he the God who knows me, but he is the God who provides everything I need.

Great Shepherd,
Thank you that you see all our needs and that you provide for us. May we run
to you first whenever we feel needy. Amen.

MIND

THE WEAPONS WE FIGHT WITH ARE NOT THE WEAPONS OF
THE WORLD. ON THE CONTRARY, THEY HAVE DIVINE POWER
TO DEMOLISH STRONGHOLDS. WE DEMOLISH ARGUMENTS AND
EVERY PRETENSION THAT SETS ITSELF UP AGAINST THE KNOWLEDGE OF GOD, AND
WE TAKE CAPTIVE EVERY THOUGHT TO MAKE IT OBEDIENT TO CHRIST.

2 Corinthians 10:4-5, NIV

Since September 11, 2001, our nation takes weapons seriously. If you've ever been in line behind someone who tried to get through airport security with nail clippers or a pocketknife, you've probably observed that security workers are on the lookout for weapons of all kinds.

In Paul's encouragement to believers, he reminds us that the weapons we need to confront evil strongholds in our lives are not weapons that we see and carry. Our battles are fought in the human heart, and our mind is sometimes where the battle rages the hardest. Throughout the Bible we are encouraged to guard our minds and examine our thoughts. How many times do anger, fear, pride, or anxiety challenge us each day? Sometimes these thoughts creep into our minds like guerilla warriors, silently, quietly, almost imperceptibly. But there they are, waiting for an opportune moment to battle with our better intentions and defeat us from being Christlike.

Paul recognizes the great danger in entertaining thoughts from the enemy. He teaches us that we can use supernatural weapons—prayer, God's Word, and his divine power—to "demolish" strongholds. We are not left to fight these battles in our mind with weapons that can't do the job. What a gift God's weapons are!

Lord Jesus, commander of the Lord's army,
I submit my mind to your Word and your authority today. Please fight and
win the battle on my behalf. In Jesus' name, amen.

COURAGE

BE STRONG AND COURAGEOUS! DON'T BE AFRAID OF THE
KING OF ASSYRIA OR HIS MIGHTY ARMY, FOR THERE IS A
POWER FAR GREATER ON OUR SIDE!   *2 Chronicles 32:7*

When my son Chad was about five or six, his nighttime slumber was sometimes interrupted by bad dreams. On those nights, I'd wake up to hear him crying or calling for me or my husband. I'd shuffle through the hallway to Chad's room and sit on the edge of his bed.

The first thing I did was listen to his fears, and then I told him that I had fears sometimes too. "When I'm afraid," I said, "I talk to God. God sees everything, knows everything, and can do anything. God is strong and God can help us."

After we talked for a while, I encouraged Chad to memorize the beginning of Philippians 4:6-7—"Don't worry about anything; instead, pray about everything." We also talked about Moses (crossing the Red Sea) and David (fighting Goliath); they had fears too, but God was faithful to give them help and courage.

Whenever our children have fearful experiences of any kind, it's important for them to know that we care about them, are willing to help them, and will consistently point them to God. Then they have opportunities to grow in faith and courage too.

Strong Father,
Thank you that you understand how weak we are, and that you share your
strength and courage with us. In the name of Jesus, amen.

WORDS

GUIDE MY STEPS BY YOUR WORD, SO I WILL NOT BE
OVERCOME BY ANY EVIL.   *Psalm 119:133*

A young man who hoped to be chosen as a steamboat pilot on the Mississippi River was nearing the end of his job interview. The interviewer, curious to discover if the young man was aware of the dangers of the river, asked if he knew where all the rocks were. The young man wisely responded, "No, sir, I do not know where all the rocks are, but I know where they *aren't*." He got the job.

As moms, we need help navigating the river of motherhood. Although each of our routes is slightly different, wisdom to know where the rocks *aren't* is available to us all. It's available in the form of words—God's words. "For the Lord grants wisdom! His every word is a treasure of knowledge and understanding" (Proverbs 2:6, TLB). God's words give us discernment for what it true, right, and lasting. His words are more valuable than gold or silver. His words are something we need to hear every day of motherhood—even after our kids have left home!

Just as we need a recipe to bake a cake or instructions to locate the correct soccer field for a child's game, we need the words of the Bible for all the situations that motherhood brings our way. We need them to help us avoid rocks like jealousy, selfish ambition, and angry outbursts. And most of all, we need them to point us to Christ, who is the source of all wisdom.

Faithful Guide,
Thanks for the gift of your Word. We would be lost without it. Amen.

MOTHERS AND WIVES

Whether it's Mother's Day or Christmas, I enjoy pondering the fact that Jesus had a mother. When we look at the New Testament accounts of the life of Christ, we don't have to search far to see the important role his mother had in his life. Over time though, her role changed. The way she handled that shifting role leaves a great example for us.

Mary's love for Jesus was obvious. She wrapped him in swaddling clothes in Bethlehem. She and Joseph fled with him to Egypt. They watched his wisdom and independence blossom. In Jesus' adult years—when Mary witnessed him turn the water into wine at a wedding—her role as a mom seemed to change. She stepped back and acknowledged his authority. She continued to follow him on his trips as he ministered to people around him. On one of those trips, when he announced that his mother and brothers were not those connected to him by flesh and blood but those who were part of the family of faith (Luke 8:21), she was presented with another aspect of her role change: in addition to being Jesus' mother, she was his disciple as well. It's obvious that she accepted that position, because she followed Jesus to his death and stood at the foot of his cross. After the Resurrection, Mary was also present in the upper room, where she waited for the Holy Spirit along with the other disciples.

When we struggle as moms, when we're unsure of our roles, when we need wisdom and help for a particular stage, it is so comforting to remember that the one to whom we pray is also one who had a mother!

Jesus,
Thank you that you understand our challenges from both a human and a
divine perspective. May we look to you for help and wisdom when we deal
with things that you observed and experienced yourself. Thank you that you
are "God with us." Amen.

WORSHIP

THE SHEPHERDS WENT BACK TO THEIR FIELDS AND FLOCKS,
GLORIFYING AND PRAISING GOD FOR WHAT THE ANGELS HAD
TOLD THEM, AND BECAUSE THEY HAD SEEN THE CHILD, JUST AS THE
ANGEL HAD SAID.

Luke 2:20

*B*efore the births of my three sons, my husband and I made lists of people we wanted to call after our babies were born. The grandmas and the grandpas were at the top of the list. Next came the aunts and uncles, and then our close friends.

Who did God choose to tell first about his son's birth? Shepherds! An angel of the Lord appeared to humble shepherds who were quietly doing their jobs—tending their sheep underneath the night sky. How encouraging! God doesn't seek people with extraordinary qualifications. His good news was—and still is—for everyone. He comes to anyone with a heart humble enough to receive him.

The joyful news announced to the shepherds was that the Savior of the world had just been born in Bethlehem, and that they could find him there, lying in a manger. As soon as that announcement was made, an army of angels sang, "Glory to God in the highest"—words that have inspired more Christmas songs for the last two thousand years than we could begin to count. This was the most joyful news ever announced in history. The humble shepherds, along with the angels, were among the first to worship and praise God for sending Jesus!

The shepherds leave us a great example for our personal worship. Worship doesn't need to wait for a church service, and it doesn't need to be complicated. It is praising God for what he's done, right where we are. May we, like the shepherds, worship God with humble hearts.

Father,
Thank you that you chose humble shepherds to praise you with the angels at Jesus' birth. We want to worship you too. In the glorious name of Jesus, amen.

HOPE

*T*he angel's announcement of the virgin birth had the word *impossible* written all over it. Mary wasn't married, she hadn't experienced sexual relations, and she was probably no older than fourteen. Furthermore, Nazareth, Mary's hometown, was an unlikely location for an important proclamation such as this. Not even mentioned in the Old Testament, Nazareth was despised by the people in Judah.

When the angel Gabriel visited Mary, he gave her a lot of information in a short amount of time. He told her that she was favored by God, that God was with her, that she would give birth to a son, and that she should name him Jesus. This would not be just any son—he would be the Son of God, and his kingdom would never end!

Mary's response provides a pattern for us to follow. She didn't say, "This is impossible!" She said, "How will this be?" In other words, how will this be possible? She understood what would happen, but she didn't understand *how* it would happen.

Are you facing an impossible situation? Do circumstances seem hopeless or insurmountable? Examine the angel's answer to Mary. The angel announced that the Holy Spirit would overshadow her, and she would experience the transforming power of God's presence. He encouraged her with news that Elizabeth, her very old cousin, was also pregnant—another seeming impossibility. With God, nothing is impossible.

As believers, we have the presence of God's Spirit, who specializes in transforming and encouraging our hearts. May we, like Mary, ask "How?" and submit to God's transforming power in our lives.

Father,
Forgive us for too often responding to difficulties with "This is impossible!"
instead of looking to you and asking, "How, God?" Thanks for your Spirit
who teaches and encourages us. Amen.

PERSEVERANCE

As a young mom, I remember coming to the end of some days feeling extremely inadequate for the job. Reflecting back on the day, I'd think of the times I'd been impatient. I'd think of times I wished I'd dropped whatever I was doing to play with the kids. Some nights, I felt so weary of waking up with a fussy baby that I wasn't sure how I would find the strength to keep going.

Perseverance keeps us going when we feel like quitting. It prompts us to stick with the task even when we'd rather run the other direction. Sheer grit and will-power are helpful in the short run, but we need something more significant to keep us going in the long run. The Bible promises a prize—or, as Galatians 6:9 expresses it, a "harvest of blessing." A harvest is a crop, a consequence, or a return on our investment.

One of my short-term prizes has been to see my sons grow in Christian character. But the long-term blessing will come someday when I—and my children—realize the prize of eternal life with Christ. Someday we will live and reign with him, and like a good farmer, I want us to enjoy the fruit of our labors!

Corrie ten Boom, a humble Dutch woman who along with her family hid Jews in her home during the Nazi invasion of Holland, had lots of opportunities to work on perseverance. Landing in a concentration camp, there were times that she felt like giving up hope. But she didn't. Corrie wrote, "When a train goes through a tunnel and it gets dark, you don't throw away your ticket and jump off. You sit still and trust the engineer."

I'm sure glad now that I didn't "jump off the train" during the toddler years. They were certainly trying (for me they were the most difficult years of child raising), but now I'm reaping some of the harvest.

> *Father of the harvest,*
> *Please help us to plant well and persevere so that we will reap a harvest of*
> *blessing. Amen.*

FRIENDSHIP

AND ELISHA SAID, "BORROW AS MANY EMPTY JARS AS YOU
CAN FROM YOUR FRIENDS AND NEIGHBORS."   *2 Kings 4:3*

*H*ave you ever gone through a time in your life when you felt lonely but found it difficult to reach out for companionship? I have. At a period in my life when I felt depressed and discouraged, reaching out felt risky. I feared what might happen if I didn't sense acceptance from the other person.

Philip Yancey and Tim Stafford see some good in this condition. They write, "I believe God created us incomplete, not as a cruel trick to edge us toward self-pity, but as an opportunity to edge us toward others with similar needs. His whole plan for us involves relationships with others: reach out to the world around us in love. Loneliness, that painful twinge inside, makes us reach out."[3]

With all the hustle and bustle of our schedules as moms, we have a fair amount of physical companionship—especially when the children are young. But it's easy to feel lonely, even when there are lots of bodies in the room, if our soul hasn't had enough opportunity to knit with a friend or companion. God built this need into us.

Think of the woman Jesus described who lost a silver coin and upon finding it rejoiced with friends. Or remember the widow ministered to by Elisha who was instructed to ask all her friends and neighbors for jars to hold the oil that was about to be miraculously multiplied. Asking her friends for their help may have felt risky and humbling, but I like to imagine the joy and excitement they all shared in the experience.

When we get to feeling lonely, we can present our need to God because he cares, sees, and provides. But we can also then call a friend or someone we'd like to get to know and put something on the calendar!

Father,
Thank you that you intend for us to need other people. Thank you that you
understand our loneliness because you experienced it yourself when you lived
on earth. May we do our part in connecting with others around us. Amen.

FRIENDSHIP

A FEW DAYS LATER MARY HURRIED TO THE HILL COUNTRY
OF JUDEA, TO THE TOWN WHERE ZECHARIAH LIVED. SHE
ENTERED THE HOUSE AND GREETED ELIZABETH.   *Luke 1:39-40*

*T*hink about your close friendships. What are some of the ingredients that make them special? My list includes common values, enjoyable companionship, mutual respect, shared circumstances, and exchanged confidences.

In Luke 1 we read that during the months before and after the births of John the Baptist and Jesus, Elizabeth and Mary formed a special friendship based first on their common values. The Bible explains that Elizabeth was obedient to God's Word. And in Mary's reaction to the angel's announcement, we see evidence of her humility, belief in God, and willingness to be his servant.

The circumstances these women shared were remarkably similar. Both women's pregnancies were announced by angels, and both were unusual—Elizabeth's because she was old, and Mary's because she was a virgin. Both women were obedient to God and were willing to be his servants.

I like how Luke described the way Mary "hurried" to the town where Elizabeth lived. That's how it is when we enjoy the companionship of another woman—we can't *wait* to share our news!

Mary and Elizabeth must have had many cups of tea and hours of deep conversation as they shared the secrets of their own experiences—the angels, the announcements, the wonder, and the pregnancies. The mutual respect between these two women was fascinating. If they had been petty or selfish women, there might have been some jealousy. But instead we find Elizabeth, who was full of God's Spirit, blessing Mary, and Mary, who was full of belief, praising God. They were truly soul mates whose souls were aligned first with God and then with each other. These two women of faith left an exquisite example of Christian friendship for us today.

> *Father,*
> *Thank you for the companionship, respect, shared circumstances, and confidences modeled in the friendship of Mary and Elizabeth. Please provide us with the blessing of Christian friends and give us grace to be the best friend we can be. Amen.*

EXAMPLE

WHEN JESUS SAW HIS MOTHER STANDING THERE BESIDE
THE DISCIPLE HE LOVED, HE SAID TO HER, "WOMAN, HE IS
YOUR SON." AND HE SAID TO THIS DISCIPLE, "SHE IS YOUR
MOTHER." AND FROM THEN ON THIS DISCIPLE TOOK HER INTO HIS HOME.

John 19:26-27

In contrast to the Roman soldiers whose job required them to be present at Jesus' crucifixion, John and Jesus' mother, Mary, were there because of love. Jesus and John had been close friends, and Mary and Jesus shared a love that few others understood. In addition to the typical memories that mothers and sons share, Mary and Jesus both knew they were part of God's plan for the world—his plan to establish relationship between God and humans.

Even as he was dying, Jesus left us an example for our own relationships: He *noticed*, *spoke*, and *provided*. Jesus *noticed* his mother and his friend. In spite of the fact that he was very near death and had been hanging on the cross for hours, he noticed. What amazing, selfless love! I sometimes fail to notice others' needs just because I am tired.

Even though it took great physical effort, Jesus *spoke*. He said to Mary, "Woman, he is your son," and to the disciple, "She is your mother." How touched Mary must have felt that Jesus was using some of his last words to remind her of how much he cared for her.

Jesus *provided* for Mary by asking John to take her home with him. Mary was a widow at that time, and Jesus exercised love and responsibility in wanting to make sure his mother had food and shelter.

Jesus' example of noticing, speaking, and providing is one we can follow in all of our friendships and family relationships.

Lord Jesus,
Thank you that even when you were close to death, you noticed, you spoke, and you provided. May we follow your example. Amen.

ANIMALS

WHAT IS THE PRICE OF FIVE SPARROWS? A COUPLE OF
PENNIES? YET GOD DOES NOT FORGET A SINGLE ONE OF THEM.
AND THE VERY HAIRS ON YOUR HEAD ARE ALL NUMBERED. SO DON'T BE
AFRAID; YOU ARE MORE VALUABLE TO HIM THAN A WHOLE FLOCK OF SPARROWS.

Luke 12:6-7

*S*parrows are common birds. To the casual observer, it may seem that a sparrow is a sparrow is a sparrow. But when I looked up *sparrow* in *North American Wildlife*, I discovered seventeen different varieties, and there are probably more. Because I am a musician, I was particularly interested in the song sparrow, which has more than thirty subspecies. Their songs often begin with a few regularly spaced notes, followed by a trill, and end with a jumble of notes. Amazingly, no two song sparrows sing exactly the same tune!

Jesus taught that God cares about each sparrow. He also taught that each of us is worth much more than a sparrow to him. Too many times we judge our worth by what we believe others think of us. That kind of thinking gets us into trouble because our value then depends on how we look, what we achieve, or how well we perform. When we look to God for our worth, we receive from him a deep sense of belonging. It gives me great comfort to know that if God cares for even the most common of birds, just think how much he cares for me!

God,
Thank you that you have given worth to everything you created. Please help us never to forget how valuable we are to you, and also how valuable our children are to you. Amen.

THANKS

THE UNFAILING LOVE OF THE LORD NEVER ENDS! BY HIS MERCIES WE HAVE BEEN KEPT FROM COMPLETE DESTRUCTION. GREAT IS HIS FAITHFULNESS; HIS MERCIES BEGIN AFRESH EACH DAY.

Lamentations 3:22-23

*I*magine that I have given you a bowl full of sand and asked you to try to find the particles of iron in it. You might look for them with your eyes or run your fingers through the sand, but you wouldn't be able to detect the iron. If, however, you took a magnet and swept it through the sand, the iron particles would be irresistibly drawn to it.

An unthankful heart is like a finger trying to sift the sand for iron—it doesn't discover God's mercies. But a thankful heart, just like the magnet, sweeps through life's circumstances and finds daily blessings from God.

I do a lot of things *daily*. I walk, shower, read my Bible, feed the cat, bring in the mail, and read the newspaper. God does many things daily too, and I tried jotting some of them down one day to prompt my thankfulness. It wasn't hard. God brought the sun up this morning. He sustained the crickets that I heard chirping. He provided the pleasant breeze I enjoyed while I was out walking. He oversaw the growth of the juicy peach I had for lunch. He brought the sun down in the evening. He gave me strength to meet the needs of the day.

A thankful heart prompts a good attitude. Because God's blessings are new every morning, it's good for us to keep our thanks current for what he supplies *each day*.

God our provider,
May we choose daily to have a grateful heart because you are faithful. Amen.

THANKS

IT IS GOOD TO GIVE THANKS TO THE LORD, TO SING PRAISES
TO THE MOST HIGH. IT IS GOOD TO PROCLAIM YOUR UNFAILING
LOVE IN THE MORNING, YOUR FAITHFULNESS IN THE EVENING.

Psalm 92:1-2

There are many ways to thank God in prayer. Here are four forms we can use and model for our children:

1. *Give thanks for provisions.* Psalm 104:13-14 says, "You send rain on the mountains from your heavenly home, and you fill the earth with the fruit of your labor. You cause grass to grow for the cattle. You cause plants to grow for people to use." We can thank God for food, breath, strength, light, encouragement, protection, and many other provisions each day.

2. *Give thanks in all situations.* First Thessalonians 5:18 urges us, "No matter what happens, always be thankful, for this is God's will for you who belong to Christ Jesus." One of my friends reminded me that the verse doesn't mean to give thanks *for* all things but *in* all things. We may not be grateful for the problem, but we thank God for what he's accomplishing in us through the problem.

3. *Give thanks for what God is doing in people's lives.* In 1 Thessalonians 1:2-3 Paul states, "We always thank God for all of you and pray for you constantly. As we talk to our God and Father about you, we think of your faithful work, your loving deeds, and your continual anticipation of the return of our Lord Jesus Christ." These are very specific areas of growth for which we can offer thanks—faithfulness, love, and hope.

4. *Give thanks in anticipation of what God will yet do.* Philippians 4:6 says, "Don't worry about anything; instead, pray about everything. Tell God what you need, and thank him for all he has done." Giving thanks to God for things yet to come indicates our trust in him.

Offer thanks for provisions, in all circumstances, for God's work in our lives, and in anticipation of what he *will* do!

> Father,
> Thanks for hope to keep going. Thanks that you are in control even when we feel off-balance. Thanks that you will be with us each day. Amen.

GOD

YOU FORMED THE MOUNTAINS BY YOUR POWER AND
ARMED YOURSELF WITH MIGHTY STRENGTH. YOU QUIETED
THE RAGING OCEANS WITH THEIR POUNDING WAVES AND
SILENCED THE SHOUTING OF THE NATIONS. THOSE WHO LIVE AT THE ENDS OF THE
EARTH STAND IN AWE OF YOUR WONDERS.

Psalm 65:6-8

My friend Ruthie just returned home from a vacation to the Canadian Rocky Mountains. When she showed me her pictures of the snowcapped mountains, colorful wildflowers, and clear-as-glass lakes, the words that came to mind were *majestic* and *glorious*.

When Jim and I and our sons take vacations to the ocean—whether it's the emerald waters of Gulf Shores, Alabama, or the aqua waves of Hallandale, Florida—our pictures prompt descriptive words like *mighty* or *awesome*.

We humans have a penchant for wonder. We are captivated by spectacular sights like a peacock spreading its wings or a porpoise leaping in the ocean. But we finite humans also need glimpses of how wonderful God is—and that's what nature gives us. I think that's why many of the words we use to describe mountains or oceans are words that the Bible uses to describe God. If the mountains and the oceans are *this* glorious, and the Bible tells us that God formed the mountains and quieted the raging oceans, God must be much more awesome than anything we could ever imagine!

Visiting the mountains or the ocean with our children gives us incredible opportunities to witness the power and majesty of God. As J. I. Packer phrased it, "The world dwarfs us all, but God dwarfs the world."

> *God of the mountains and the oceans,*
> *Thanks for the beauty you created in the world, all of which points back to*
> *you. Amen.*

FOOD

IS ANYONE THIRSTY? COME AND DRINK—EVEN IF YOU HAVE
NO MONEY! COME, TAKE YOUR CHOICE OF WINE OR MILK—
IT'S ALL FREE! WHY SPEND YOUR MONEY ON FOOD THAT DOES NOT GIVE
YOU STRENGTH? WHY PAY FOR FOOD THAT DOES YOU NO GOOD? LISTEN, AND I
WILL TELL YOU WHERE TO GET FOOD THAT IS GOOD FOR THE SOUL!   *Isaiah 55:1-2*

On a bright, sunny day, our family hiked up a trail in the Colorado Rocky Mountains to Agnes Veil Falls. The falls were situated way back off the road, and it was quite a climb to get there. But the reward was worth it! With the sun high in the deep blue sky, we heard the rushing water before we saw it. Great torrents of sparkling water cascaded over the jagged rocks, coming from melting snow above our ten-thousand-foot perch.

My family loves to vacation close to water. There is something refreshing about being near it. But water is more than just good recreation; it's essential for our bodies. We may be able to live without food for some days, but not without water. That helps explain why Isaiah likened our thirst for water to our soul's thirst for God.

Sometimes we try to quench our hunger and thirst for God with other things, even good things. But Isaiah reminds us that it is only in finding the Lord that we will find satisfaction. And Jesus, in the Gospel of John, reminds us that he himself is the Living Water. God's Word and God's Son water our hearts, bringing life to us and satisfying us with God himself.

> Lord,
> Thank you that you have provided a way to quench the thirst in our souls.
> May we daily drink in all the refreshment that it provides and be fruitful for
> you. In the strong name of Jesus, amen.

FOOD

It's noteworthy that Jesus was born in a town whose name means "house of bread"—Bethlehem. Most of us eat bread. Whether we bake it or buy it, bread is a staple food. It's basic to life.

Imagine what it would have been like to be on the hillside when Jesus blessed the five loaves of bread and two fish, multiplying them to feed thousands of hungry people. The miracle was amazing, but also amazing was the response of the crowd. After seeing Jesus provide them with food, the people wanted to make him king. Why? Not because they believed he was the Messiah, but because they thought he could provide them many material things. The people were so caught up in having their immediate physical needs met that they missed the real significance of the event—that Jesus *is* the bread of life. Jesus knew that they desired the bread more than they desired him.

May we not miss the truth that we need Jesus as our staple—that the Bread of Life who was born in the town called "house of bread" wants to be our spiritual food each day of our lives.

O little town of Bethlehem, how still we see thee lie!
Above thy deep and dreamless sleep the silent stars go by.
Yet in thy dark streets shineth the everlasting light;
The hopes and fears of all the years are met in thee tonight.[4]

Father,
Thank you that you are the bread of life and that you can meet all our hopes and fears. Amen.

HEART

ABOVE ALL ELSE, GUARD YOUR HEART, FOR IT IS THE
WELLSPRING OF LIFE.   *Proverbs 4:23, NIV*

*W*hat is a *wellspring*? It is the source of a stream or a spring, the point where something springs into being, or the place where things are created. What a fitting picture of our hearts, where thoughts, attitudes, and actions are initiated. The verse above begins with a weighty warning. More than anything else, we must guard our hearts. Not coddle, pamper, or indulge—but *guard*. When I guard something, I protect it, watch over it, or take necessary precautions to keep it safe.

Our hearts determine our true character. Are we pursuing purity or evil? Are we headed toward maturity or rebellion? The Bible teaches us that the most important thing we can do is to love God with our *whole hearts*—which are undivided and fixed on Jesus. Then we must guard them. Notice the common thread in these verses:

> *Be careful then, dear brothers and sisters. Make sure that your own hearts are not evil and unbelieving, turning you away from the living God. (Hebrews 3:12)*

> *Draw close to God, and God will draw close to you. Wash your hands, you sinners; purify your hearts, you hypocrites. (James 4:8)*

> *Fix your thoughts on what is true and honorable and right. Think about things that are pure and lovely and admirable. Think about things that are excellent and worthy of praise. (Philippians 4:8)*

We guard our hearts by running *to* God and running *away* from sin. Then we have a wellspring full of good things!

> *Father,*
> *May we take the warning of your Word seriously. You are gracious to fill and cleanse our hearts when we come to you, but we must make choices to run from sin. Thank you for your Holy Spirit, who helps us. Amen.*

PRAYER

HANNAH WAS IN DEEP ANGUISH, CRYING BITTERLY AS SHE
PRAYED TO THE LORD.

1 Samuel 1:10

*H*ave you ever experienced times of grief, bitterness, or anguish, when you felt as though you were slipping? Hannah did. Back in the Old Testament book of 1 Samuel (1:1–2:21), we learn that Hannah was married to Elkanah, a Levite priest. He also had a second wife, named Peninnah. Each year the combined families made a trip to the Shiloh tabernacle, and each year the same thing happened: Elkanah celebrated his sacrifices by giving gifts to Peninnah and each of her children, but Hannah received only one for herself because she had no children. The Bible tells us that Peninnah laughed at Hannah's barrenness, making Hannah cry so much that she couldn't eat.

One evening in Shiloh, Hannah went over to the tabernacle. Out of her bitter grief and anguish, she cried out to the Lord. In the process of praying, she endured even *more* taunting because the priest mistook her sorrow for drunkenness! But something amazing happened after she poured out her heart to God. The priest gave her a blessing of peace, and after she left the tabernacle, she ate and her face was no longer downcast. After worshipping God together, the families went home, and Hannah became pregnant. We find Hannah's beautiful song of praise in 1 Samuel 2:1-10.

What's the lesson for us? In our heartache or anguish, we can cry out to the Lord, acknowledging that he is God and we are not. We can pour out our souls—grief, bitterness, and all. And after we bring him our requests, we can get on with our lives and worship God, thankful that he hears us.

Father,
Thank you for examples of women like Hannah, who experienced some of the
same feelings of sorrow we have from time to time. Thank you that we can
express our emotions to you and that you give us the grace and strength to
stand up and move ahead. Thanks for your answers to our prayers. Amen.

CHOICES

When I was a student at Moody Bible Institute, I sang in the Moody Chorale. Whether we toured in England, Miami, Scotland, or Syracuse, we began each concert by singing:

> *Guide me, O Thou great Jehovah,*
> *Pilgrim through this barren land;*
> *I am weak, but Thou art mighty;*
> *Hold me with Thy powerful hand.* [5]

Weak. Perplexed. Uncertain of how to choose. Do you ever feel that way? I do. When we encounter challenging circumstances, where do we go for help with our needs and our choices?

Where we look for guidance says a lot about our character. Some people turn to the local bar or a palm reader, but a wise choice would be a pastor or a counselor—a mature person who believes in and loves God and his Word. When we have serious choices to make, we need wise counselors. One of my sons is deciding which college to attend; his guidance counselor at school is a great resource person. One of my friends is navigating through some challenges in her marriage; her marriage counselor is a huge source of help.

Human counselors are helpful, but *Jesus* is the foremost counselor in the world. He knows us, loves us, is patient with us, and encourages us. And—as any good counselor—he doesn't protect us from problems, but he equips us to face them with honesty and courage.

When you feel weak or uncertain, grab on to Jesus' hand and ask *him* to help you choose.

> *Loving Counselor,*
> *Thank you that you are the wisest counselor and guide we could ever have. In our weakness, please be our strength. Amen.*

FEAR

CAST ALL YOUR ANXIETY ON HIM BECAUSE HE CARES FOR
YOU.

1 Peter 5:7, NIV

*F*irst Peter 5:7 was one of the earliest Bible verses I memorized as a child, and it is a verse I have taught to my children. But even when we have *memorized* a verse from the Bible, it doesn't mean we have yet learned the lesson and seen it worked out in our lives. God wants us to cast all our anxiety on him. Other words for anxiety are fear, apprehension, doubt, fretfulness, panic, nervousness, or uncertainty. We've all been there, haven't we? Perhaps you're there now because your husband lost his job, you are caring for an ailing parent, or you're worried that your child might get into an accident.

One of the reasons God permits difficulties in our lives is to present us with opportunities to learn and exercise lessons of faith. We read in Mark 4 that Jesus had been teaching his disciples when they got into a boat together on the Sea of Galilee and promptly encountered a violent storm. Even though (1) Jesus had told the disciples they were going to the other side of the lake, (2) he was with them, and (3) he was calm, they still cried out to him, "Teacher, don't you even care?" (v. 38). We sometimes do the same thing!

After Jesus calmed the storm, he spoke to his disciples about the unbelief in their hearts. He was more concerned about the problem *within* them than the problems *around* them. This God who is in control wants us to cast (throw, fling, heave, or thrust) our anxieties and fears on him because he cares for us.

God who is in control of everything,
Thank you that you welcome our worries and fears. Thank you that you are
not indifferent to our cries, but that you care for us. Amen.

TIME

MOSES SAID TO GOD, "SUPPOSE I GO TO THE ISRAELITES AND
SAY TO THEM, 'THE GOD OF YOUR FATHERS HAS SENT ME TO
YOU,' AND THEY ASK ME, 'WHAT IS HIS NAME?' THEN WHAT SHALL
I TELL THEM?" GOD SAID TO MOSES, "I AM WHO I AM. THIS IS WHAT YOU ARE
TO SAY TO THE ISRAELITES: 'I AM HAS SENT ME TO YOU.' "
Exodus 3:13-14, NIV

*W*hat do the following questions have in common?

1. When is dinner?
2. How old are you?
3. Is your term paper due next week?

Time. We all measure time, and we all know that time passes, but it's impossible to say exactly what time is. One dictionary defines it as "a nonspatial continuum in which events occur in apparently irreversible succession from the past through the present to the future."

That prompted me to look up the word *continuum*: "A continuous extent, succession, or whole." It seems to me that God is the continuum—God who mentioned his full name in the Bible only once: "I am who I am."

God spoke his name to Moses when Moses was out with his sheep one day and encountered a burning bush. Moses approached because he thought it was curious that the bush was on fire but didn't burn up. Then God spoke to him from the bush, asking him to go to Pharaoh and lead the Israelites out of Egypt. Although that display of God's power took place many years ago, God hasn't changed. Hebrews 13:8 reminds us that God is the same yesterday, today, and forever.

As we face challenges in our families, it's very comforting to know that God is the I AM. What difficult situations are you facing in your piece of God's continuum? It's good to be reminded of the glory and power of the "I AM" God who is always the same, accomplishing his purposes in us as we look to him.

God,
When Moses struggled to understand how you were going to accomplish your
plans through him, you came alongside him and showed him how powerful
and mighty you are. We struggle with some of the same questions at times.
Please encourage us with your Word and with your presence, so we will be
equipped to do your Kingdom work, beginning in our home. Amen.

Humility

MARY RESPONDED [TO ELIZABETH], "OH, HOW I PRAISE THE LORD. HOW I REJOICE IN GOD MY SAVIOR! FOR HE TOOK NOTICE OF HIS LOWLY SERVANT GIRL, AND NOW GENERATION AFTER GENERATION WILL CALL ME BLESSED. FOR HE, THE MIGHTY ONE, IS HOLY, AND HE HAS DONE GREAT THINGS FOR ME. HIS MERCY GOES ON FROM GENERATION TO GENERATION, TO ALL WHO FEAR HIM. HIS MIGHTY ARM DOES TREMENDOUS THINGS! HOW HE SCATTERS THE PROUD AND HAUGHTY ONES! HE HAS TAKEN PRINCES FROM THEIR THRONES AND EXALTED THE LOWLY. HE HAS SATISFIED THE HUNGRY WITH GOOD THINGS AND SENT THE RICH AWAY WITH EMPTY HANDS. AND HOW HE HAS HELPED HIS SERVANT ISRAEL! HE HAS NOT FORGOTTEN HIS PROMISE TO BE MERCIFUL. FOR HE PROMISED OUR ANCESTORS— ABRAHAM AND HIS CHILDREN—TO BE MERCIFUL TO THEM FOREVER." *Luke 1:46-55*

Humility jumps from the page as we read what Mary said (or sang) to her cousin Elizabeth, reflecting on God's promise to make her the mother of the Messiah. What a beautiful snapshot of a humble heart. Notice some of the ingredients of humility included in her song:

1. Humility involves moving the focus off ourselves. Mary didn't praise herself—she praised God. She spoke of him as her Savior and Lord and acknowledged that he was mighty, holy, and merciful.
2. Humility doesn't mean insecurity. Mary acknowledged God's power and love, which she had felt in her own life.
3. Humility shows us where we fit in the big picture. Mary understood that she was part of a much bigger plan than just her days on earth. She knew she was involved in a design that God had for the world. It's easy for us to get caught up in our own agenda and forget that we are here to serve.
4. Humility springs from our innermost being. Mary saw that things are not always as they appear. What's important to God is not the position we hold before our peers, but rather the state of our inmost thoughts about God. That's where humility begins.

Father,
Thank you for the beautiful song that Mary sang in praise to you. May we learn from her example of humility and be an example to our children of a mom who praises you out of an overflowing heart. Amen.

TIME

IF YOU NEED WISDOM—IF YOU WANT TO KNOW WHAT
GOD WANTS YOU TO DO—ASK HIM, AND HE WILL GLADLY TELL
YOU. HE WILL NOT RESENT YOUR ASKING.

James 1:5

I recently saw a cartoon in a women's magazine showing a little boy sitting at a kitchen table. His mother was serving him a meal, and the little boy was saying, "Mom, where did you work before you worked for Dad and me?"

I both smile and cringe at that little boy's question. I smile because, like the mom in the cartoon, I spend a lot of time serving my family, and most of the time I enjoy it. I cringe because I dislike the times when I feel like a slave to everyone else's needs and wants, having little time left over for the things I like to do. After being a mom for twenty some years, I have to admit that finding a balance is a constant challenge. I've had times when I felt overly responsible for my family and didn't take enough time to be healthy myself. At other times I was so involved in "good" things that in my busyness I neglected some of my family's needs.

For some years I have been praying daily for wisdom to know how to use my time, and it has helped immensely! I don't claim to have found the perfect balance, but when I talk to God about my schedule each morning, I'm much more conscious of making wise choices since I've already thought and prayed about it. And when things don't go well, I reevaluate and ask God for more wisdom.

Father,
Thank you that we can come to you for wisdom. Please give us help in balancing the many responsibilities of motherhood. Amen.

TIME

REMEMBER YOUR CREATOR IN THE DAYS OF YOUR YOUTH.

Ecclesiastes 12:1, NIV

Jay Thomas, the college pastor at my church, recently shared an illustration he had heard from Alistair Begg. Imagine someone told you that each day he was going to place $86,400 in your bank account. Your job was to spend all of it every day, and anything you didn't spend by midnight would be lost. You'd probably spend a fair amount of time figuring out what you wanted to do with the money! Jay went on to say that even though most of us will never have $86,400 deposited in our bank accounts each day, every one of us is given 86,400 seconds of time to use each day. The question is, *How are we spending all those seconds?*

I am indebted to Sunday school teachers and youth workers who encouraged me to memorize Bible verses like the one above. I am also indebted to my parents, who built healthy opportunities, disciplines, and boundaries into my life, all of which helped me to use my time wisely. Now that I'm an adult, I'm no longer accountable to my parents for how I use my time, but I am accountable to God. And although I don't have the youth of my childhood, I don't yet have the limitations mentioned in Ecclesiastes 12:2-5 of dim eyes, trembling limbs, loss of teeth, or deafness to music. So, if God wills, I still have time to remember my Creator and honor him throughout the 86,400 seconds of each day I have left!

> *Little drops of water, little grains of sand,*
> *Make the mighty ocean and the pleasant land.*
> *So the little minutes, humble though they be,*
> *Make the mighty ages of eternity.* [6]

Father,
Please help us to make each second of the day count for you and your Kingdom. In Jesus' name, amen.

FOOD

"YOU DIDN'T HAVE ENOUGH FAITH," JESUS TOLD THEM.
"I ASSURE YOU, EVEN IF YOU HAD FAITH AS SMALL AS A MUSTARD
SEED YOU COULD SAY TO THIS MOUNTAIN, 'MOVE FROM HERE TO
THERE,' AND IT WOULD MOVE. NOTHING WOULD BE IMPOSSIBLE." *Matthew 17:20*

My family has this running joke about mustard. I like the plain variety, but everyone else in the family (my husband and three sons) likes Grey Poupon. So I shop for both kinds and try not to take it personally when they call mine the "sissy mustard."

Here's a life lesson you can teach your kids the next time they squeeze mustard on a hot dog: Even though the mustard seed is extremely small, the mustard plant can reach a height of fifteen feet. From the seeds of the mustard plant we can make a sauce (plain or spicy) to use on our favorite sandwiches.

When Jesus lived on earth, he taught his disciples spiritual truths by talking about everyday things. Mustard came up several times in his teaching. In Matthew 17 Jesus grieved over the lack of faith he saw in his disciples and told them that if they had faith as small as a mustard seed, they would do great things for God.

Great faith has very small beginnings. It begins with opening ourselves to God. When we come to him and expose our dark hearts to the light of his grace and truth, the roots of our lives are forced down into the soil of his amazing love. Then, miraculously, just as green shoots of the mustard plant come out of the ground and grow to heights of four to fifteen feet, we see shoots of faith—maybe even large ones—appearing in our lives.

Father,
Thank you for teaching us big lessons through small things. May we place our faith in you and see growth take place in our lives. Amen.

FOOD

"WHAT CAN I DO TO HELP YOU?" ELISHA ASKED. "TELL ME,
WHAT DO YOU HAVE IN THE HOUSE?"   *2 Kings 4:2*

*J*ust a little oil," the widow told the prophet Elisha. "That's all that I have in my
house." She had lost her husband, and now she feared that her creditor might
come and take away her two sons as slaves. If the Israelites around this widow had
been following the Levitical laws, the woman and her sons would have been provided for. Instead, sadly, their situation seemed to be headed in the wrong direction.

When the widow was feeling totally helpless, Elisha asked her two questions:
"How can I help you?" and "What do you have in your house?" I appreciate the
graciousness of Elisha's inquiries. He wanted to help, and he began with what she
had. His questions were not patronizing or pessimistic but compassionate and
hopeful.

Elisha then told her to borrow many jars from her neighbors. Next she was to
pour oil into all the borrowed containers. Then the oil flowed until she and her
sons filled the last jar! She sold the oil and had enough money to pay off her credi-
tors and support her family.

Like the widow, we sometimes face situations that we think might have,
could have, or should have headed in a different direction. When the painful real-
ities of life leave us feeling needy or even hopeless, we can run to God for his gracious compassion and words of hope. He is still the God who sees and provides.

Father,
Thank you that you saw the widow's situation and provided for her. Thank
you that you see us today and that we can run to you and ask you to provide
for us. Amen.

ANIMALS

TAKE A LESSON FROM THE ANTS, YOU LAZYBONES. LEARN
FROM THEIR WAYS AND BE WISE! EVEN THOUGH THEY HAVE NO
PRINCE, GOVERNOR, OR RULER TO MAKE THEM WORK, THEY LABOR
HARD ALL SUMMER, GATHERING FOOD FOR THE WINTER. *Proverbs 6:6-8*

Although ants are small, they are very wise. They almost make us look lazy. They work day and night, they store up food, and they build their mounds three or four times higher (comparatively speaking) than the Egyptian pyramids are to us. When ants are sick, they care for each other, and in the winter they eat what they saved in the summer.

Ants have one of the most elaborate social organizations in the animal world. Thousands of ants live in a communal nest, each one having its own task to perform. These workers gather, make, and store food for both the adults and the larvae.

Living near fields of grain and carrying seed into their private storehouses, the ants described in Proverbs 6 are harvester ants. When cold weather comes, these ants swarm together and hibernate. They have enough food stored up during the winter to last until the next harvest. God gave ants an amazing ability to solve problems and plan ahead. For example, if the grain they stored gets wet, they haul it out to dry in the sun.

These tiny creatures are included in the Bible as examples for us. They are busy, they plan ahead, and they work together. The next time you're out on a walk with your child and you see an ant, take the opportunity to discuss some of the lessons we can learn from these tiny creatures.

God,
Thank you that we learn important lessons about life from some of your tiniest creatures. Like the ants, help us to be diligent in the work you've given us to do. Amen.

EXAMPLE

AND YOU YOURSELF MUST BE AN EXAMPLE TO THEM BY
DOING GOOD DEEDS OF EVERY KIND. LET EVERYTHING YOU
DO REFLECT THE INTEGRITY AND SERIOUSNESS OF YOUR TEACHING.

Titus 2:7

After urging (nagging?) my sons for many years to do things like brush their teeth, say please and thank you, and use their napkins at the dinner table, I'm pleased to report that I have no reason to remind them anymore—at twenty-six, twenty-four, and eighteen they do these things automatically.

There's something very rewarding about seeing young children remind someone else to follow the behavior we've urged them to practice. I remember seeing this happen one spring day when Chad was three or four. We had just returned home from the grocery store, and Chad had a leftover piece of bread in his hand. While I was in the kitchen putting away groceries, I heard Chad start to cry outside. I ran to the back door and saw that the piece of bread he had set down in his wagon was now being carried off in the beak of a big, black crow! As I walked over to console Chad, he put his hands on his little hips and yelled up to the crow, "Birdie, what do you say?" I'm not sure whether Chad wanted to hear a "thank-you" or an "I'm sorry," but clearly this crow needed to say something!

As moms, we are models, patterns, and illustrations to our children. The habits we display to them, for better or for worse, are the habits they will most likely adopt in their own lives. And then—sometimes in surprising ways—they will model those habits for others. "The first gift we can bestow on others," wrote Thomas Morell, "is a good example."

Father God,
Thank you for the Bible, which teaches us how to live with integrity. May we
imitate you, so that our children will have good examples to follow. In the
name of Jesus, amen.

ATTITUDE

May the Lord bless you and protect you. May the Lord smile on you and be gracious to you. May the Lord show you his favor and give you his peace.

Numbers 6:24-26

The words we choose and the attitudes we use in speaking to our children about their future hold tremendous influence on how they will think and act as adolescents and adults.

If a child grows up hearing positive words of confidence, encouragement, and blessing from a parent, those words will stick when the child begins to have those inevitable questions about his or her worth during adolescence.

The opposite is also true. If children grow up hearing negative words of criticism, nagging, and sarcasm from a parent, those words will also stick—sometimes for the rest of their lives. The way we reflect on who our children are now and who we think they will become has more impact on them than we probably realize.

Gary Smalley and John Trent write, "When it comes to predictions about their future, children are literalists—particularly when they hear predictions from their parents, the most important people from an earthly perspective in their lives."[7]

Here are a few ways to encourage our children and help them see God's blessing for their lives:

- When a child has had a bad day at school, decide together to pray daily that God will bring some special blessing or encouragement to that child's life, thanking him together when he does.
- As a son or daughter displays characteristics that will be admirable in marriage or fatherhood or motherhood someday, point them out, and then remind him or her that you pray regularly for his or her future spouse, wherever that person may be.
- Pray the verses above for your child at bedtime or when he or she is leaving on a trip.

Father,
In the same way that we leave a church service encouraged by a hopeful benediction, please help us to encourage our children to see your blessing and hope in their lives. Amen.

REVERENCE

THOSE WHO FEAR THE LORD ARE SECURE; HE WILL BE A
PLACE OF REFUGE FOR THEIR CHILDREN.   *Proverbs 14:26*

The benefits of reverence for God don't stop with us—they are passed down to our children in some very unique ways. We're taught in this proverb that if a parent fears, or reverences, the Lord, she has a secure spiritual fortress. The refuge and protection of that fortress will be experienced by her children as well.

A fortress includes walls around a city to protect it from enemy attacks. Back in Bible times these walls were fifteen to twenty-five feet thick and twenty-five feet high. On top of these walls, towers were built at regular intervals, giving defenders a good viewpoint from which they could counter an attack. The outside walls were often protected by a moat that made direct assault almost impossible. A city inside a fortress typically had only one gate—two at the most—keeping security very tight. Since no city could last long without an adequate water supply, fortified cities were generally built near rivers or springs.

When we choose to reverence God by trusting him, spending time in his Word, and obeying what we're learning, he becomes our spiritual fortress. Our walls are built thick against temptation, we become wise about what we need to look out for, and our water supply—refreshment from God—is unending. Even if we did not experience growing up in a family fortress of faith and security, we can choose, through reverence for God, to have that security for ourselves and for our children.

Father,
Oh, how we need to be protected. Thank you that you want to be our fortress.
May we choose to reverence you so we will experience security for ourselves and
for our children. Amen.

MOTHERS AND WIVES

WE WILL NOT HIDE THESE TRUTHS FROM OUR CHILDREN
BUT WILL TELL THE NEXT GENERATION ABOUT THE GLORIOUS
DEEDS OF THE LORD. WE WILL TELL OF HIS POWER AND THE MIGHTY
MIRACLES HE DID.

Psalm 78:4

*M*ax Jukes lived in New York. He did not believe in Christ or in Christian training. He refused to take his children to church, even when they asked to go. He has had 1,026 descendants; of those, 300 were sent to prison for an average term of thirteen years, 190 were public prostitutes, and 680 were admitted alcoholics. His family, thus far, has cost the state in excess of $420,000. They made no measurable contributions to society.

Jonathan Edwards lived in the same state at the same time as Jukes. He loved the Lord and saw that his children were in church every Sunday as he served the Lord to the best of his ability. He has had 929 descendants, and of these 430 were ministers, 86 became university professors, 13 became university presidents, 75 authored good books, and 7 were elected to the United States Congress. One was vice president of his nation. His family never cost the state one cent but has contributed immeasurably to the life of plenty in this land today.[8]

What kind of heritage are we leaving for *our* children? Down the road, we'd all like to pass on some kind of monetary inheritance or a few pieces of furniture that will hold sentimental value. But we'd be wise to focus more on the inheritance with a value that cannot be measured.

Will we pass down a love for God and his Word; an example of truth, love, and mercy; and a grateful heart? These are the most valuable gifts we can give.

Father,
In our busy days as moms, please help us to think ahead to the kind of inheritance we wish to leave for our children. Help our words and actions to match.
Amen.

SECURITY

> HE WHO FEARS THE LORD HAS A SECURE FORTRESS, AND
> FOR HIS CHILDREN IT WILL BE A REFUGE.   *Proverbs 14:26, NIV*

*H*ave your children ever made "forts" inside or outside your home? My kids have had forts at sleepovers made out of blankets duct-taped to tables and chairs. They have also built snow forts. Their largest project was a three-level tree fort in the backyard that took three summers to build.

A fort for our kids is a cozy place where they can play, but a fort or fortress in the military sense is much more substantial—it's a place of strength and security. God tells us that when we respect and acknowledge him, *he* is our fortress. Because of God's presence in our lives, the strength and security he provides can be experienced in any location.

Corrie ten Boom was a Dutch woman whose parents feared the Lord. During the Nazi invasion of Holland during World War II, Corrie's family hid Jewish people in their home so those people wouldn't be sent to the Nazi concentration camps. Sadly, Corrie and her family ended up in those very camps because of their help to the Jews. Corrie's fortress—her refuge in God—was sometimes experienced in her father's watch shop, sometimes on a cramped train ride, sometimes in the secret room of their home, and sometimes in the bunks of a concentration camp. Her fortress wasn't a physical dwelling. Rather, it was the security of her relationship with God.

We often spend time and money on our actual dwelling places, which has some value. But how much more important it is that we teach our children to be in awe of God, who is our ultimate security and fortress in all of life—our refuge wherever we may be.

Father,
Thank you that the security we have in you doesn't depend on where we are or where we live. Thank you that we carry it in our souls. Amen.

FATHER TO THE FATHERLESS, DEFENDER OF WIDOWS—THIS
IS GOD, WHOSE DWELLING IS HOLY.   *Psalm 68:5*

*T*he Bible teaches us that when we put our faith in God, we become children of God, and God is our Father. The dictionary defines a father as a man who begets, raises, or nurtures a child, and God is faithful to do all of that for us. He created us, gives us his nature, provides for us, and loves us deeply. Some women, myself included, have gratefully experienced those things from their earthly father; but sadly, not every woman's father has lovingly raised or nurtured her. Some women have experienced their father's death, abandonment, or abuse.

It is challenging for these women to understand the God of the Bible. But since injustices, large or small, cross all our paths from time to time, we are wise to realize that God's Word, not our own package of life experiences, must frame our faith.

Michael Horton writes, "While in practice we cannot help but be influenced in our views of God's fatherhood by our earthly experiences, the Good Father can heal our broken images."[9]

Reading God's Word helps us see that we can run to God confidently because he is our faithful Father. (If you struggle with understanding God's father-love for you, reading John 10:1-30 may give you hope and encouragement.)

Father,
Thank you that as we read your Word, it frames our faith and helps us to understand what a wonderful Father you are to us. Amen.

ANIMALS

HE GIVES POWER TO THOSE WHO ARE TIRED AND WORN
OUT; HE OFFERS STRENGTH TO THE WEAK. EVEN YOUTHS
WILL BECOME EXHAUSTED, AND YOUNG MEN WILL GIVE UP. BUT
THOSE WHO WAIT ON THE LORD WILL FIND NEW STRENGTH. THEY WILL FLY HIGH
ON WINGS LIKE EAGLES. THEY WILL RUN AND NOT GROW WEARY. THEY WILL
WALK AND NOT FAINT.
Isaiah 40:29-31

*E*agles are majestic birds, and even though certain types are considered endangered species, the God who created them and gives life to them knows the address of every eagle alive. Eagles build their nests in trees or cliffs—high places that are inaccessible—and they add to their nests each year, using sticks, weeds, and dirt. Sometimes a nest ends up weighing over a thousand pounds, and some nests have been reported to measure up to fifteen feet deep! In these deep nests, a female eagle hatches two eggs, only one of which usually survives to be an adult.

A mother eagle carries her eaglet on her back until it masters the art of flying. Moses spoke of this picture from nature to remind us how God cares for his people: "Like an eagle that rouses her chicks and hovers over her young, so he spread his wings to take them in and carried them aloft on his pinions" (Deuteronomy 32:11). God has probably delivered us from more than we could ever imagine.

An eagle can soar for hours at a time while searching for prey. It rides wind currents, rarely moving its wings. God promises us that if we hope in him, he will provide some of that soaring time as well. It would be great if we could soar all the time, but that's not how life works. Sometimes we soar, sometimes we run, sometimes we walk, and sometimes we stumble and fall. But the Lord promises to replenish our strength as we hope in him.

God who knows every eagle's address,
Thank you for the beauty of an eagle's flight. As we hope in you, please help
us to soar; but help us to look to your strength during times of weariness as
well. Amen.

FRIENDSHIP

A FRIEND IS ALWAYS LOYAL, AND A BROTHER IS BORN TO
HELP IN TIME OF NEED. *Proverbs 17:17*

God's Word reminds me that knowledge alone is not enough for spiritual growth. I also need the grace of friendships.

When I consider my close friendships, three things come to mind. First, mutual love. None of us is perfect, so we're not looking for perfection, but it's important to respect some of our friend's qualities. Second, mutual trust. Friends can rely on each other to keep confidences, help out when needed, and do what they say they're going to do. Because friendships are built on mutual respect and trust, God warns us in Proverbs 22:24-25, "Keep away from angry, short-tempered people, or you will learn to be like them and endanger your soul." Third, shared conversations and experiences. Whether funny and lighthearted or deep and serious, we accumulate memories of sharing and caring. Of course, having each experienced the common denominator of God's love and grace adds an eternal element to our friendships.

The book *A Confident Woman* defines a friend like this: "A friend is someone to whom I do not have to explain myself. Such a friendship offers unspeakable comfort. Friendship can also be redemptive, for friends can act as mediators of God's presence and invite us into the embrace of God's grace."[10]

Over the seasons of our life, it's good to look for a balance in friendships. Are we frequently on the giving end? Are we frequently on the receiving end? It's healthy for us to experience some of both.

One of our roles as moms is helping our children learn to develop healthy friendships. We can do this by modeling strong relationships, by praying for their friendships, and by guiding and encouraging them to make healthy choices for themselves—one choice at a time.

Father,
Thank you for blessing us with redemptive friendships. Help us trust you to bring these relationships into our lives in your time. Amen.

ENCOURAGEMENT

*E*ncouraging words stimulate our spirits. They give us a boost, brighten our day, and strengthen us for our tasks. Wow! All of that can be accomplished with a few encouraging words.

The other day my husband told me how much something I said had encouraged him. A few weeks ago I'd said, "I never take it for granted that we can talk about anything and everything. Our relationship feels as comfortable to me as an old pair of slippers." Apparently, those twenty-or-so words meant more to him than I had realized.

When Moses' leadership over the children of Israel was coming to a close, God asked him to encourage Joshua—God's choice for a new leader. Part of God's plan for equipping Joshua for leadership was accomplished through Moses' encouragement. That is still God's plan in our families today. What abundant opportunities we have in our homes to encourage our husbands and our children! Does your husband travel? Tuck a few cards in his suitcase—one for each day he'll be gone. And don't be fooled by age—even high school boys enjoy getting notes in their lunches! "Kind words," said Mother Teresa, "can be short and easy to speak, but their echoes are truly endless."

Father,
Thank you for people who have encouraged us. Help us to be encouraging to
our families and friends. Amen.

WORK

WORK HARD AND CHEERFULLY AT WHATEVER YOU DO, AS
THOUGH YOU WERE WORKING FOR THE LORD RATHER THAN
FOR PEOPLE.

Colossians 3:23

Three bricklayers were hired to help build St. Paul's Cathedral in London. A curious bystander approached them and asked what they were doing. The first bricklayer responded, "I'm laying bricks—I'm making money!" The second bricklayer said, "I'm laying bricks—I'm a third-generation bricklayer. My grandpa was a bricklayer, my dad was a bricklayer, and now I'm a bricklayer too!" The third bricklayer, who had the bigger picture in mind, stepped back, looked up, and responded, "I'm assisting Sir Christopher Wren in building a great cathedral!"

Perhaps some of us can relate to those bricklayers. If a bystander came along and asked us what we were doing, we could respond, "I'm changing diapers and feeding a baby." Or, "I'm driving my kids all over town to their activities!" But a mom who has the bigger picture in mind might reply, "I'm assisting God in raising a young man or a young woman who will grow up to love and obey him."

When we complain about the drudgery of changing diapers or chauffeuring kids across town, we may have lost sight of the bigger picture. Oh, that we could step back and say, "I'm assisting God in raising my child to be a future leader!"

> Father,
> It's easy to lose the big picture, especially on a hectic day. Please help us to honor you as we raise our children. In the strong name of Jesus, amen.

FAITH

IT WAS BY FAITH THAT RAHAB THE PROSTITUTE DID NOT
DIE WITH ALL THE OTHERS IN HER CITY WHO REFUSED
TO OBEY GOD. FOR SHE HAD GIVEN A FRIENDLY WELCOME
TO THE SPIES.

Hebrews 11:31

*R*aising three boys who are becoming handsome young men brings with it the responsibility of building into their lives a godly desire for purity. Many years ago one of my very young sons announced that he wanted to marry me and live in our house when he grew up. Although I felt flattered, I knew that someday he would begin to notice pretty young women from other families. He has! Through the years, we've encouraged our sons to choose girls who value purity and avoid girls who behave seductively.

Why, then, do we find Rahab—a prostitute—praised in Hebrews for her faith? What is she doing on that list of heroes?

When Joshua was commanded to conquer the Promised Land (Joshua 6), the first city on the list was Jericho. It had walls at least twenty-five feet high and twenty feet wide! When Joshua sent two spies to Jericho, they found safety and lodging at Rahab's home right on the walls. Rahab was so convinced that the God of Israel was going to destroy her city that she put her hope in the spies—and their God— risking death as a traitor. Rahab's faith was significant to God because it led her to obey. "Only he who believes is obedient," wrote Dietrich Bonhoeffer, "and only he who is obedient believes."

God doesn't care what our past looks like. He can wash away our sins and give us hearts that love him fully and obediently. He is looking for faith—like Rahab's—that believes God can and will do the impossible.

Lord Jesus,
Give us the gift of daily faith. We believe that through your awesome power we can be free to live obediently in your care. Amen.

Obedience

AT THIS, JOSHUA FELL WITH HIS FACE TO THE GROUND IN
REVERENCE. "I AM AT YOUR COMMAND," JOSHUA SAID. "WHAT
DO YOU WANT YOUR SERVANT TO DO?"

Joshua 5:14

*A*re you up against a situation in your life that feels hopeless? Are you discouraged and tempted to give up? Before Israel's conquest of the walled city of Jericho, Joshua and the Israelites must have felt the same way. But they made several good choices.

The first thing Joshua did was to humble himself before God and commit to following God's plan. Too many times when I face a problem, my first step is to draw up my own plan. This *appears* to help, but in the long run it is like putting a bandage over a wound that needs more serious attention.

Joshua took God seriously. God said that he had delivered Jericho, along with its king and fighting men, over to Joshua and the Israelites. Would I have believed that statement if I had been there? Joshua and the Israelites chose to trust God for the impossible. Although God's plan required patience, they weren't going to be delivered through sitting back and relaxing—there was some work to be done!

Their reverence for God and their faith in him prompted their ultimate obedience. They paid amazing attention to detail, including trumpets of rams' horns, marching for seven days, and circling seven times around the city on the seventh day—usually quietly, but the last time with a shout. There was no room for laziness or cynicism.

When we humble ourselves in prayer, trust God for the impossible, and obey the details, we will see God's victory over the enemy in our lives and the lives of those we love.

Father,
Thank you for the example of Joshua, who humbled himself, trusted you, and
obeyed you. Please help us to do the same as we face our own challenges.
Amen.

COURAGE

"WE OFFER OUR OWN LIVES AS A GUARANTEE FOR YOUR
SAFETY," THE MEN AGREED. "IF YOU DON'T BETRAY US, WE
WILL KEEP OUR PROMISE WHEN THE LORD GIVES US THE LAND."

Joshua 2:14

I remember seeing flannel-graph pictures of Rahab when I heard the Bible story told as a young child. At the time, I didn't understand that she was a harlot, but I was fascinated by the scarlet rope hanging from her window. Joshua sent two spies to Jericho, and Rahab secretly housed them and then hid them on her roof under stalks of flax. Later Rahab lowered the two spies down the outside wall through the window of her house. She was a woman of courage, as she took great risk in hiding the spies. As a result of her help, she and her family were later spared death when the Israelites conquered Jericho.

It's interesting that Rahab, who lived in a pagan culture, called God "the Lord" in her conversation with the spies: " 'I know the Lord has given you this land,' she told them. 'We are all afraid of you. Everyone is living in terror' " (Joshua 2:9).

Rahab was not saved from physical or spiritual destruction because of her character or her works. Rather, she was saved through her faith. Any woman who has had major struggles with character or behavior can find great hope and encouragement from the life of Rahab. She was a sinner who was saved through her faith, and she proved her faith by courageously risking her life to protect God's people, eventually bringing her family to belief in God. She even became part of the ancestry of Jesus (Matthew 1:5)!

Father,
To trace Rahab back in Christ's ancestry is encouraging to us, because it
demonstrates that people with a sinful past can be transformed. Thank you for
her example of courage, which was born through faith in you. Amen.

MIND

BUT THIS IS THE NEW COVENANT I WILL MAKE WITH THE
PEOPLE OF ISRAEL ON THAT DAY, SAYS THE LORD: I WILL PUT
MY LAWS IN THEIR MINDS SO THEY WILL UNDERSTAND THEM, AND
I WILL WRITE THEM ON THEIR HEARTS SO THEY WILL OBEY THEM.

Hebrews 8:10

*I*n Old Testament times God's laws were written on stones, but the stones did not provide the power to live them out. God promised blessings to those who memorized God's words and taught them to their children, and the people who chose to do so experienced the wisdom and influence that his truth provides. But having God's truth written in their minds and hearts was not something humans could experience until Jesus provided a new covenant through his death on the cross.

Christian moms have a special understanding of this principle. We realize that it is our responsibility to teach our children God's Word and to guide them with God's principles. But as they grow older and mature, we pray that they will build a personal relationship with God, through Christ, so that his Spirit will write truth in their minds and hearts. A law from the outside may guide a person, but it can never *change* him or her. For our behavior to change, God's truth must become part of our inner life, and that can happen only when God's Spirit lives inside us.

This principle about heart change is illustrated in a story about two caterpillars crawling across the grass. When a butterfly flew over them, they looked up, and one nudged the other, saying, "You couldn't get me up in one of those things for a million dollars!" It took an internal change before the caterpillars could fly, and that's necessary for us too. Changes that could never happen from the outside begin to take place when God's laws are written on our minds and hearts!

Father,
Thank you that when we enter into a relationship with you through Jesus
Christ, your laws are written on our minds and in our hearts. Please help us to
be obedient to the promptings of your truth through the help of your Spirit.
Amen.

GOD

What do we do when we make something? If we make a cake with our children, we cause it to exist by combining all the ingredients, mixing them, and then baking. If we make a piece of pottery, we shape some clay with our hands or a machine. If we make laws, we institute or establish them.

When God made heaven and earth, he introduced the wonderful process of creativity. He caused things to happen. He shaped. He established. He brought life into existence. He caused matter to assume specific functions and act in specific ways.

But there's a huge difference between what we make and what God made. When we make a cake or a piece of pottery, we start with ingredients, but God made something out of nothing. I love the questions God asked Job in Job 38:4-7 (TLB): "Where were you when I laid the foundations of the earth? Tell me, if you know so much. Do you know how its dimensions were determined, and who did the surveying? What supports its foundations, and who laid its cornerstone, as the morning stars sang together and all the angels shouted for joy?" It's quite clear that God is God, and we are not!

When we encounter challenges and difficulties in our lives, how comforting and encouraging to realize that we can run to our Creator—the one who can make something out of nothing—asking him to bring order to our sometimes chaotic existence here on earth.

Father,
Thank you that heaven and earth are full of your glory! Thank you for giving
us abilities to be creative with things that you brought into being. We know
that you alone can bring order to our existence here on earth. Amen.

TRUTH

JESUS TOLD HIM, "I AM THE WAY, THE TRUTH, AND THE
LIFE. NO ONE CAN COME TO THE FATHER EXCEPT THROUGH ME."

John 14:6

Imagine that you and your children are taking a hike in Colorado. You come upon a wide river, and another hiker tells you that there is only one bridge, down the river a mile or so. Will you stomp off in disgust and complain that it's unfair that there's only one bridge, or will you be grateful that there *is* a bridge, and use it to cross over?

Imagine that your child is struggling with a serious illness. You've tried every medication and treatment possible short of surgery, and now your child's doctor tells you that surgery is the only remaining option. Will you look for a surgeon who has specialized training in the area of your child's illness, or will you choose a person off the street?

The way of truth in these two situations seems obvious to us. But when it comes to matters of faith, we are not always so quick to see the truth. Many people today fight the reality of absolute truth as though it were an enemy. To be deemed "narrow-minded" is to be considered ignorant, it seems. But the reality is that truth *is* narrow. How comforting for me to know that God is truth. He's the author of truth, and the closer we get to him, the more we live truly and truly live. We trust him with our lives because he's the only one who *really* knows what life is all about.

Father,
Thank you that to know you is to know truth. Amen.

CHRISTMAS

AS HE CONSIDERED THIS, HE FELL ASLEEP, AND AN ANGEL OF THE LORD APPEARED TO HIM IN A DREAM. "JOSEPH, SON OF DAVID," THE ANGEL SAID, "DO NOT BE AFRAID TO GO AHEAD WITH YOUR MARRIAGE TO MARY. FOR THE CHILD WITHIN HER HAS BEEN CONCEIVED BY THE HOLY SPIRIT. AND SHE WILL HAVE A SON, AND YOU ARE TO NAME HIM JESUS, FOR HE WILL SAVE HIS PEOPLE FROM THEIR SINS." *Matthew 1:20-21*

To think that the Creator of the universe was about to be born of a peasant virgin on cold, hard stable ground is astonishing. If I had been given the job of orchestrating Jesus' arrival on earth, I would have planned something grand. But God's designs often include humble reversals.

All the way through the Bible, we read of godly men and women whose lives were turned upside down for the sake of God's plan to deliver good news to mankind. Abraham was asked to leave his homeland, and he eventually became the father of many nations. Joseph was transplanted to Egypt, eventually rising from the pit to a high position of leadership. Moses was floated down the river in a basket to escape death by the king, and he was eventually raised by the king's daughter. Ruth's husband died, but she later remarried and became the great-grandmother of King David.

The entrance of Jesus into our human existence was one of the greatest reversals of all time. It didn't seem to make sense. Jesus—the Prince—was born into the world as a pauper. Just like all of God's truth, this example of humility gives us great encouragement. Over the course of our lives, we may experience difficult reversals. Even when they don't seem to make sense to us, we can be grateful that God sometimes uses them in our lives as part of his plan to deliver good news to mankind.

Lord Jesus,
Thank you that you didn't shun the reversal of taking on human flesh and dying for our sins. When painful reversals happen in our lives, may we run to you for help and eventually accept them as part of your good plan. Amen.

GOD

JOSEPH IS A FRUITFUL TREE, A FRUITFUL TREE BESIDE A
FOUNTAIN. HIS BRANCHES REACH OVER THE WALL. HE HAS BEEN
ATTACKED BY ARCHERS, WHO SHOT AT HIM AND HARASSED HIM. BUT HIS
BOW REMAINED STRONG, AND HIS ARMS WERE STRENGTHENED BY THE MIGHTY
ONE OF JACOB, THE SHEPHERD, THE ROCK OF ISRAEL. MAY THE GOD OF YOUR
ANCESTORS HELP YOU; MAY THE ALMIGHTY BLESS YOU WITH THE BLESSINGS OF
THE HEAVENS ABOVE, BLESSINGS OF THE EARTH BENEATH, AND BLESSINGS OF THE
BREAST AND WOMB.   *Genesis 49:22-25*

*A*lmighty (*El Shaddai*) is one of the names given to God in the Old Testament. It
means "sufficient and mighty," acknowledging God as a source of blessing. This
name for God appears in the accounts of two particular Old Testament characters, Joseph and Ruth, who led very difficult lives.

I suppose it's not too hard to think of God as sufficient, all-powerful, and a
source of blessing on sunny days when we're healthy, there's money in the
checking account, and our kids are doing well. But what about the gloomy days
when it feels like the rug has been pulled out from underneath us?

Joseph was left in a pit and traded for money by his brothers, taken to a foreign country, falsely accused, and sent to jail. And yet he acknowledged God's
power and later experienced his blessings—wisdom, a high position of influence, responsibility, the ability to interpret dreams, a wife and children, relief
from famine, and a miraculous reunion with his brothers and father that only God
could have orchestrated.

Ruth didn't have it easy either. Her husband and father-in-law died, leaving
her and her mother-in-law as widows who struggled for existence. But after
Ruth chose to stay with her mother-in-law, God blessed Ruth with a husband and
eventually gave them a son who became the grandfather of King David!

The next time we face a difficult day and struggle with seeing God as sufficient, all-powerful, and full of blessing, perhaps we would be wise to read the
stories of Joseph and Ruth and be encouraged anew by God's almighty power.

Father,
Thank you that you left us with accounts of people who dealt with difficult
circumstances and found your mighty power to be more than just enough.
They were blessed abundantly, and we are too. Amen.

COURAGE

"SEE," NAOMI SAID TO HER, "YOUR SISTER-IN-LAW HAS
GONE BACK TO HER PEOPLE AND TO HER GODS. YOU
SHOULD DO THE SAME." BUT RUTH REPLIED, "DON'T ASK ME TO
LEAVE YOU AND TURN BACK. I WILL GO WHEREVER YOU GO AND LIVE WHEREVER
YOU LIVE. YOUR PEOPLE WILL BE MY PEOPLE, AND YOUR GOD WILL BE MY GOD."

Ruth 1:15-16

*W*oven throughout the Bible are stories of courage—stories of seemingly un-important people who accomplished great things in God's strength. God's plans and purposes are carried out from one generation to another with amazing twists, turns, and surprises, and Ruth was part of one of those plans.

A woman who had grown up in Moab, Ruth married a Jewish man, Mahlon, one of the sons of Elimelech. Elimelech, his wife, Naomi, and their two sons had left Israel to escape a famine, and while they were in Moab, both sons married Moabite women. Sadly, Elimelech and both sons died, leaving Naomi and two daughters-in-law as widows. Naomi decided to return to her hometown of Bethlehem, assuming Ruth and Orpah would prefer to stay in Moab. But because of Ruth's love for Naomi, she insisted on going along.

An industrious woman, Ruth gleaned grain that had been dropped by harvesters in the field of Boaz, bringing it back to Naomi to bake bread. When Boaz found out who Ruth was, he offered her much more than the leftovers. He was kind to her because of her kindness to Naomi.

In God's plan, Ruth and Boaz ended up marrying, and a few generations later Ruth became the great-grandmother of King David. Because she had the courage to leave her homeland, accompany her mother-in-law back to Israel, and work to provide for her mother-in-law, God blessed her life. What a beautiful story of love and courage!

Father,
Thank you for the intricate way your plans unfold from one generation to
another. Thank you that we can read these stories in your Word and be
reminded of your great love and faithfulness. May we have faith to believe
that you are weaving your purposes into our lives and courage to obey. Amen.

COURAGE

THEN THE BABY'S SISTER APPROACHED THE PRINCESS.
"SHOULD I GO AND FIND ONE OF THE HEBREW WOMEN TO
NURSE THE BABY FOR YOU?" SHE ASKED.

Exodus 2:7

Courage is found not only in older people but also in young people. Consider Miriam, the sister of Moses. Moses' mother, Jochebed, decided to do a very bold thing. In order to protect Moses from being killed by Pharaoh's soldiers, she wove some reeds into a small basket. Perhaps Miriam wondered what her mother was making—until she found out that the basket would cradle her baby brother as he floated down the river. Miriam probably watched her mother weep as she kissed her infant son and laid him in the basket, putting it into the water. I can only wonder what Miriam thought and felt as she stood on the riverbank, watching from a distance.

You know the rest of the story. Pharaoh's daughter found the baby when she went to the river to bathe, and Miriam ran to her, asking if she should find a Hebrew mother (her own!) to nurse the baby. What a brave thing for a child to do. The courage she exercised as a young girl no doubt prompted her own growth in faith. Imagine all the times that she and Jochebed must have rehearsed that story together through the years. Later in the book of Exodus we read that Miriam led the children of Israel in a song of praise after their miraculous crossing of the Red Sea.

It's often painful for mothers to sit back and watch their children struggle through difficult situations. We would much rather protect them from pain or risk. But as we see in Miriam, courage can spring from childhood difficulties, resulting in personal faith and leadership down the road.

Father,
When we know or sense that our children are struggling with some difficulty,
please give us great wisdom as moms to know how much to guide them, how
much or how little to say, and when to stand back and wait to see you work in
their hearts and lives. Amen.

ENCOURAGEMENT

> THEN I HEARD AGAIN WHAT SOUNDED LIKE THE SHOUT OF
> A HUGE CROWD, OR THE ROAR OF MIGHTY OCEAN WAVES, OR
> THE CRASH OF LOUD THUNDER: "HALLELUJAH! FOR THE LORD
> OUR GOD, THE ALMIGHTY, REIGNS."
>
> Revelation 19:6

My eleven-year-old son was seated next to me in our van when the tape we were listening to began to play the "Hallelujah Chorus" from Handel's *Messiah*. As Jordan took off his seat belt and tried to stand up, we laughed! *Everyone* knows that you stand when you hear the "Hallelujah Chorus," right? But not everyone knows of Handel's discouragement leading up to that composition.

George Frederic Handel's father was a barber who was determined that his son would become a lawyer. In spite of the fact that Handel loved music as a child, his father forbade him to take lessons. That changed when a duke who heard nine-year-old Handel play the organ strongly encouraged the father to give the boy formal music training.

Although he was enormously gifted as an organist and composer, Handel didn't have an easy existence. He fell in and out of favor with changing monarchs, dealt with unpredictable audiences, and was so deeply in debt that he thought he might end up in prison. Terribly discouraged, Handel was ready to retire from public life when he received a libretto taken entirely from the Bible. At the same time, he was given a commission from a Dublin charity to compose a work for a benefit performance.

Handel began composing, and after twenty-four days he completed 260 pages of a manuscript titled *Messiah*. One writer commented that the music and message of *Messiah* "has probably done more to convince thousands of mankind that there is a God . . . than all the theological works ever written."[11]

Just because we're discouraged doesn't mean God can't use us!

God who sees the whole picture,
It's easy for us to give up and lose heart when we're discouraged. It's easy for our children to want to give up. Help us run to you and remember that many people who have contributed to expanding your Kingdom were at some point discouraged. Amen.

HUMILITY

BUT HE SAID TO ME, "MY GRACE IS SUFFICIENT FOR YOU,
FOR MY POWER IS MADE PERFECT IN WEAKNESS."

2 Corinthians 12:9, NIV

When I encounter problems and difficulties in my life, too often my initial approach is to work hard at being strong. I like to see myself as a person who is resilient physically, mentally, emotionally, and spiritually. But I have discovered that even the best of my strength is no match for many of the challenges of my life here on earth.

I'm also tempted to focus on myself when I'm in a crisis. I feel sorry for myself, spend time thinking about myself, and try to protect myself. But when I spend great amounts of time thinking about myself and not a lot of time thinking about God, I'm in trouble.

The apostle Paul is a great example to me of a humble person. God was able to use Paul tremendously to further his kingdom, and he didn't do it because Paul was strong. God told Paul in the verse above, "My grace is sufficient for you, for my power is made perfect in weakness."

Hebrews 11 reminds us of Gideon, Barak, Samson, Jephthah, David, and the prophets, who because of their faith saw their weakness turned into strength (see verse 32). God can use us when we realize we're *not* strong on our own and admit our weakness before him. We ask him to take our frail offerings and use them to increase *his* kingdom, not ours.

Father,
The message we get in our culture today is, "Be strong!" But you tell us that
we're wise to admit our weakness, run to you, and wait to see your power and
strength worked out in our frail beings. May our children see your strength
because they see us turning to you in times of need. Amen.

GRACE

FOR IT IS BY GRACE YOU HAVE BEEN SAVED, THROUGH
FAITH—AND THIS NOT FROM YOURSELVES, IT IS THE GIFT
OF GOD.

Ephesians 2:8, NIV

Grace is the favor and kindness of God shown to us in spite of the fact that we
don't deserve it. Grace cannot be purchased or earned because it is a *gift*. But like
any gift, it can't be appreciated or experienced unless it is accepted. When we accept God's grace by faith, we become victorious, generous, courteous, and
strong.

We are *victorious* because we have already been raised from the grave of sin
and seated with the risen Lord. Sadly, we often forget that we have received this
gift of victory over our sinful nature.

We are *generous* because we have received God's gift of grace, and we want to
follow his example. I remember one year when my dad shared one of his bonuses
from work with all four of us children. He didn't have to, but in his gratitude he
wanted to. When we receive God's grace, we feel the same way—we want to
share it with others.

God's grace makes us *courteous*. Because God has not been critical and angry
with us, we avoid being that way with others.

Finally, God's grace makes us *strong*. The beauty of God's strength is that it is
made perfect in our weakness. God's strength was shown through giving sight to
a blind man and through David's small sling, and it can be exhibited in our weakness when we present ourselves as vessels of his grace.

Because of God's gracious gift to us—his Son—we can share the blessings of
victory, generosity, courtesy, and strength in our interactions with our children,
our husbands, and our friends. God's grace makes us *rich*!

Father,
The more we get to know you, the more we appreciate your grace. Thank you
for your indescribable gift! Amen.

HUMILITY

DON'T BE SELFISH; DON'T LIVE TO MAKE A GOOD IMPRESSION
ON OTHERS. BE HUMBLE, THINKING OF OTHERS AS BETTER THAN
YOURSELF. . . . YOUR ATTITUDE SHOULD BE THE SAME THAT CHRIST JESUS
HAD. THOUGH HE WAS GOD, HE DID NOT DEMAND AND CLING TO HIS RIGHTS AS
GOD. HE MADE HIMSELF NOTHING; HE TOOK THE HUMBLE POSITION OF A SLAVE
AND APPEARED IN HUMAN FORM. AND IN HUMAN FORM HE OBEDIENTLY HUMBLED
HIMSELF EVEN FURTHER BY DYING A CRIMINAL'S DEATH ON A CROSS.

Philippians 2:3, 5-8

Throughout the Bible, we're reminded that "the Lord supports the humble, but he brings the wicked down into the dust" (Psalm 147:6). That same thought appears in Psalm 18:27—"You rescue those who are humble, but you humiliate the proud." Clearly, God hates pride and values humility.

If we want to improve our sewing, cooking, decorating, or parenting skills, thousands of books are available to help us. But if we want to learn how to be humble, where do we go? I've never run across a book titled *Humility 101* in my local bookstore.

The Bible tells us that the place to go—the person to look at—is Jesus. There's no better role model for any of us. In Philippians 2, we discover that humility begins with an attitude—one that looks up at God and up at other people. When we look at our holy, powerful God, there's only one direction to look, and that's up! Our biggest problem is that we don't spend enough time looking at him. And when we look at other people, we sometimes look down, but that's not the right direction.

When the attitude of humility is present in our hearts, the actions of humility seem to follow. Instead of demanding, we begin serving. Instead of clinging to our rights, we begin thinking about others. Even though Jesus was God, he didn't demand and cling to his rights. Instead, he took the humble position of a slave, to the point of death on a cross—for us. By looking at Jesus' attitude and actions, we find the only perfect example of humility.

Father,
Each day we face many opportunities to practice humility, but it doesn't come
naturally to us. Please help us look to your example and your strength and
make the choice to serve others. In Christ's name, amen.

FEAR

WHO ARE THOSE WHO FEAR THE LORD? HE WILL SHOW
THEM THE PATH THEY SHOULD CHOOSE. *Psalm 25:12*

What are some of your fears as a mom? Through twenty years of motherhood, I've experienced plenty of my own. The first one I remember was, "How will I know what to *do* with this little person when I bring him home from the hospital?" Apparently, God helped me figure it out, because Chad grew up safely and presently teaches high school physics. Now it's *his* turn to figure out what to do with a whole classroom.

While I was pregnant with my second child, I feared that I wouldn't be able to love that child as much as I loved my firstborn. I smile now because as soon as I started taking care of Nate, my fear dissolved in the middle of my busyness. The third time around, I feared that I wouldn't be able to squeeze in much one-on-one time with our youngest child. Now that the first two have graduated from college, my husband and I spend all kinds of one-on-one time with Jordan. He gets more time with us than the other two ever did.

Although my fears were probably common, they weren't particularly helpful. But one fear is—the fear of the Lord. The Bible teaches that fearing the Lord doesn't mean being scared of him or avoiding him. Instead, it's seeing God for who he is and responding to him with reverent and affectionate obedience. Part of fearing him is presenting our fears to him—fears about our kids, schedules, husbands, health, jobs, and relationships. When we trust him with our fears, we discover that he is faithful to help us choose good paths. Fearing God helps us to put our other fears in proper perspective.

Father,
Thank you that we can trust you with our fears. Help us always to respond to
you with the reverence and obedience you deserve—and may that give us the
right view of our lives. Amen.

PRAYER

O MY PEOPLE, TRUST IN HIM AT ALL TIMES. POUR OUT
YOUR HEART TO HIM, FOR GOD IS OUR REFUGE.   *Psalm 62:8*

What do we do when we're up against a problem that's far bigger than anything we can handle? Some problems in life are solvable—like the time I turned on my blender when the top wasn't securely fastened. It made quite a mess in my kitchen, but in ten or fifteen minutes I had it cleaned up. Larger problems that can't be solved either quickly or easily—like giving birth to a baby who has severe medical problems—are often accompanied by overwhelming feelings.

I remember a time I encountered a life experience that I neither wanted nor understood. All I knew was that I felt a lot of pain and sadness. I decided to get alone for one day of thinking and praying. I wasn't really alone, though. I have special memories of God's presence and strength washing over me as I paced the floor with open Bible in hand, reading accounts of people in the Bible who met up with seemingly impossible circumstances. The common denominator in their prayers was that they meditated on things God had done in the past, like parting the waters of the Red Sea and protecting Daniel in the lions' den.

We too are wise to begin our prayers with reminders of things God has done in the past. That helps answer the question we all ask when we hit a snag—"Is God *really* in control?" As we remember what he has done in the past and cry out to him for help in our present situation, our hearts are stirred to trust him.

Father,
Thank you for the honesty of the psalmists and other writers in the Bible who
were good examples for us of how to pray even when our hearts are heavy.
May we pour out our longings to you and rehearse your faithfulness to us.
Amen.

Fear

He said, "Listen, King Jehoshaphat! Listen, all you
people of Judah and Jerusalem! This is what the Lord
says: Do not be afraid. Don't be discouraged by this
mighty army, for the battle is not yours, but God's."   *2 Chronicles 20:15*

Jehoshaphat, king of Judah, was about to face a combined army of the Moabites and the Ammonites, two ancient enemies of Israel. When Jehoshaphat received news from some of his men that enemy troops were advancing, he was alarmed.

When we sense an army of trouble coming upon us—whether it's financial difficulties, health problems, or a crisis in our family—what is our reaction? Panic, fear, anger? These are normal human reactions, but we run into trouble if we get stuck there. Any of those reactions, left unchecked, will only add to the confusion and intensity of the problems confronting us.

Notice some excellent choices Jehoshaphat made in this situation (see 2 Chronicles 20:1-30):

- He resolved to ask the Lord for guidance.
- He encouraged the people to fast and pray.
- In front of the people, he rehearsed who God is and what he had done in the past. Then he asked for God's help, admitting that the people did not know what to do, but that their eyes were upon God.

Through a prophet, God told the people not to be discouraged or afraid, pointing out that the battle was not theirs—it was his. They then gave thanks and praise to God even before they saw who was going to win the battle.

The amazing conclusion is that the enemies were thrown into confusion, killing each other, and Jehoshaphat and his people were saved! When faced with trouble or crisis, may we, like Jehoshaphat, remember to pray and praise, waiting to see what God will do.

Father,
Thank you for examples of people who, though fearful and imperfect like we
are, made some wise decisions to trust you. Thanks for lessons from the past
that remind us that you are faithful. Amen.

HOPE

WE WAIT IN HOPE FOR THE LORD; HE IS OUR HELP AND
OUR SHIELD. IN HIM OUR HEARTS REJOICE, FOR WE TRUST IN
HIS HOLY NAME. MAY YOUR UNFAILING LOVE REST UPON US,
O LORD, EVEN AS WE PUT OUR HOPE IN YOU.

Psalm 33:20-22, NIV

*H*ave you ever waited for something very important? For a parent to know Christ? For a child to complete cancer treatments? For a husband who has strayed from God's truth to return? Waiting is difficult. The Old Testament character Joseph spent a fair amount of his life waiting. I've often wondered what his life was like—first in the dry well where his brothers dumped him before they sold him to Ishmaelite traders, and then as he waited again before he arrived in Egypt and was sold to Potiphar, one of Pharaoh's officials. But the Bible tells us that God was with Joseph and that Joseph experienced success in all that he did.

Even when he was falsely accused and sent to prison, Joseph knew God showed him extra kindness through the prison warden. After two more years of waiting, Joseph was not only called out of prison to interpret Pharaoh's dream, but he was put in charge of Pharaoh's palace and ultimately the whole land of Egypt. Joseph was eventually reunited with his family in a miraculous way that only God could have arranged! (Read more of Joseph's story in Genesis 37, 39–45.)

Was Joseph waiting on his brothers? The Ishmaelites? Potiphar? Yes, but he was also waiting on God. The influence and even forgetfulness of some of those individuals was all part of God's larger plan for the world. Are you experiencing a time of waiting in your life? Remember, we're not only waiting on people or a process—we're waiting on God.

God who sees and provides,
Waiting sometimes feels hopeless and pointless. But we find encouragement in
seeing your faithfulness to other people who waited on you. May we experience
your unfailing love as we put our hope in you. Amen.

PRAYER

So we have continued praying for you ever since
we first heard about you. We ask God to give you a
complete understanding of what he wants to do in
your lives, and we ask him to make you wise with spiritual wisdom.

Colossians 1:9

Mary, one of my friends from church, hosted a prayer time one fall for moms whose children had gone off to college. We enjoyed a wonderful time of praying together for the needs of our children. What made it particularly special was that Mary suggested we use Scripture to pray back to God some of the specific ways he wants us all to grow to be more like him.

I have found this to be helpful, not only in my prayers for my children, but also in prayers for my husband, myself, and my friends and extended family. Below I've listed several verses we can pray on behalf of our children. As you spend time in God's Word, I'm sure you will find many more prayer verses. But these are good for a start.

I pray that your love for each other will overflow more and more, and that you will keep on growing in your knowledge and understanding. (Philippians 1:9)

And now I entrust you to God and the word of his grace—his message that is able to build you up and give you an inheritance with all those he has set apart for himself. (Acts 20:32)

God of the Bible,
Thank you for leaving us your Word of Truth. Thank you that your words add power to our prayer. Amen.

LIGHT

I COULD ASK THE DARKNESS TO HIDE ME AND THE LIGHT A
ROUND ME TO BECOME NIGHT—BUT EVEN IN DARKNESS I CANNOT
HIDE FROM YOU. TO YOU THE NIGHT SHINES AS BRIGHT AS DAY. DARKNESS
AND LIGHT ARE BOTH ALIKE TO YOU.   *Psalm 139:11-12*

One of my favorite childhood memories was taking a summer trip to the Shaffers' cottage in Lake Nebagamon, Wisconsin. The two highlights of the week were going to Bridgeman's for ice cream and visiting the town dump. "The dump?" you might ask. "What's so great about visiting the town dump?"

The town dump was a good place to see bears. After dark, we parked our car a short distance from the dump, turned off the headlights, and listened for sounds of animal life. When we heard rustling or banging, the driver of the car would turn on the lights so we could see what was going on. Most of the time all we saw was raccoons, but sometimes the car beams exposed bears. Great excitement! In the darkness, we had no idea what we were hearing, but when the lights of the car shone in front of us, we were able to spot the animals. It was the light that made things clear.

On this earth, we experience both light and darkness—depending on the time of day and season of the year. But God is not limited by darkness. He dwells in light and he sees us all the time, no matter where we are. He not only sees us but he knows everything about us. His light is always on, because he *is* light. How comforting—especially for a child—to know that we can never be lost to God.

Father,
Thank you for the security that your light brings to our lives. Amen.

Faith

Fight the good fight of the faith. Take hold of the eternal life to which you were called when you made your good confession in the presence of many witnesses.

1 Timothy 6:12, NIV

During times in our lives when we're struggling with doubts about God, it's good to remember that doubt is not the same as unbelief. Alister McGrath writes, "Unbelief is the decision to live your life as if there were no God. It is a deliberate decision to reject Jesus Christ and all that he stands for. But doubt is something quite different. Doubt arises within the context of faith. It is a wistful longing to be sure of the things in which we trust."[12]

It's comforting to learn that doubt is a natural part of growing in faith because faith is not easy. To fight for faith is not only to strive vigorously *for* it but also to struggle *against* our adversary, the devil. First Timothy 6:12 is set in a chapter that instructs us to do three things—flee, follow, and fight. We are to flee from pride, the love of money, and false teachings; follow after righteousness, godliness, faith, love, endurance, and gentleness; and fight *for* faith and *against* the world, the flesh, and the devil.

A mom who is depressed, whose husband is involved in addictive behavior, or whose child is hanging out with unwholesome friends has plenty of doubts and struggles—she's clearly in a fight. As we fight against the world, the flesh, and the devil through the power of God's Word and Spirit, we "take hold of . . . eternal life"—we grab it, setting our hope not on fleeting things but on God who gives eternal life and is himself hope.

Father,
Please give us strength as we fight the good fight of faith. Thank you that you have promised you will always be with us. Please help us to grab hold of your promises when doubts rise in our minds and hearts. Amen.

PEACE

You will keep in perfect peace all who trust in you, whose thoughts are fixed on you! Trust in the Lord always, for the Lord God is the eternal Rock.

Isaiah 26:3-4

Some years ago our family rented a cottage at Honey Rock Camp in northern Wisconsin. The cottage was far off the beaten path—down a gravel road, off a smaller dirt lane, and nestled amidst some fragrant pine trees. Set on a little rise, the cottage overlooked a small river and came complete with a rope tied to a tree limb above—perfect for swinging and plunging into the river. What an ideal place to take three young boys!

In the early morning and at dusk the river was especially still. At times it became a mirror, reflecting the trees, sky, and everything else above it. The river was the perfect picture of peace.

Many times in life, things aren't as serene as the river outside our cottage. The storms of life churn up the water, we begin to feel overwhelmed, and it may seem as though we'll be carried away by strong currents.

But Jesus said, "I am leaving you with a gift—peace of mind and heart. And the peace I give isn't like the peace the world gives. So don't be troubled or afraid" (John 14:27). He said this shortly after he reminded Philip that those who had seen him had really seen the Father. Jesus was identifying himself with the Great Jehovah, God the Father.

When the rivers of our lives are churning, Jesus reminds us that we must fix our thoughts on him—on his strength, love, and faithfulness. We must choose to rest in his care and good plans for our lives.

The hymn writer Frances Havergal put it this way:

> *Like a river glorious is God's perfect peace,*
> *Perfect, yet it floweth fuller ev'ry day,*
> *Perfect, yet it groweth deeper all the way.*
> *Stayed upon Jehovah, hearts are fully blest—*
> *Finding as He promised perfect peace and rest.* [13]

Lord God,
Thank you for the peace you offer us as we trust in you. Help us to keep our thoughts fixed on you. In Jesus' name, amen.

CONTENTMENT

*C*ontentment should be the hallmark of the person who has put his or her affairs in the hands of God.[14] To be content, we must have an accurate picture of who God is and who we are. Looking at the relationship between a shepherd and his sheep helps us to better understand that picture.

Throughout the Bible God is described as the Good Shepherd, and people are sometimes likened to sheep. King David was a boyhood shepherd himself, and he knew that sheep are very needy. The lot in life of any one sheep depended on the shepherd who cared for it. A shepherd could be kind, thoughtful, and wise, or he could be mean, inconsiderate, and irresponsible. When we see God as our shepherd, we realize that we have the very best care available. Our shepherd is all-powerful and all-knowing. He never sleeps, and he cares about us individually because he gave us life and sustains us.

In order to be content, sheep must have freedom from fear, tension, aggravation, and hunger. It is the job of the shepherd to provide these freedoms by driving away predators, providing food and water, and keeping the sheep from other harm. God provides us with his Spirit to minister security, peace, and hope, and he gives his Word to feed us.

When we as needy people understand that we gain the very presence of God in our lives through the Holy Spirit, we realize the contentment that God intends for each one of us. He *is* the shepherd of our souls, and only he can provide true contentment.

Father,
Thank you that you describe yourself as our shepherd. We're grateful that we can find our contentment in you. Amen.

PEACE

I WILL LIE DOWN IN PEACE AND SLEEP, FOR YOU ALONE,
O LORD, WILL KEEP ME SAFE.

Psalm 4:8

When I was in my early thirties, my husband traveled a fair amount for his job. I was not accustomed to being alone at night and found that I wasn't sleeping very well. When I mentioned my situation to a friend, she related an experience I'll never forget.

Theo and her husband were missionaries to West Africa—Americans living in a foreign culture. Security was an issue even when her husband was around, but when he traveled on occasion, she felt apprehensive at night. One morning while her husband was away on a trip, she awoke to discover that she had left a door to the courtyard not only unlocked but *open* the night before. After checking through the house and realizing that everything was all right, she reasoned that if God could take care of her and keep her safe when the door was open overnight, then she need not worry about being home alone. From then on when her husband was gone at night, she remembered Psalm 4:8.

We read in Mark 4 that Jesus and his disciples were in a boat on the Sea of Galilee when a fierce storm suddenly came up. In the middle of the storm, Jesus was able to continue napping. Why? Because he knew that God would care for him.

Are you experiencing storms in your life? Are any of your children struggling at school or with friends? Remember that God wants us to come to him for refuge. He is our peace. He is our security.

Father,
Instead of worrying and being fearful, may we run to you when we feel inse-
cure, realizing that you want to give us your peace. Amen.

WISDOM

BUT THE WISDOM THAT COMES FROM HEAVEN IS FIRST OF ALL
PURE. IT IS ALSO PEACE LOVING, GENTLE AT ALL TIMES, AND
WILLING TO YIELD TO OTHERS. IT IS FULL OF MERCY AND GOOD
DEEDS. IT SHOWS NO PARTIALITY AND IS ALWAYS SINCERE. AND THOSE WHO ARE
PEACEMAKERS WILL PLANT SEEDS OF PEACE AND REAP A HARVEST OF GOODNESS.

James 3:17-18

We identify a wise person the same way we identify a tree—by the fruit he bears. A tree is identified by the lemons, cherries, or grapefruit it bears. A wise person is identified by the following:

- *Purity*. Pure morals come from being cleansed by Christ's blood. When we receive Christ's purity, we set aside sensuality, pride, and covetousness. Purity of devotion is a result of our focus on God. We concentrate on serving and pleasing *him*.
- *Peace*. This is not a passive quality, meaning we avoid conflict and become doormats to whatever our children or husbands want. Rather, it means having a calm, tranquil spirit, which comes from a close relationship with Christ.
- *Consideration*. We treat others the way we'd like to be treated. This means that sometimes we put others' needs first.
- *Submission*. This involves a willingness to yield to another. A wise person is open to reason and doesn't always need to be right.
- *Mercy*. This is compassion that is not just thought about but is acted out toward another person at times when it would be easier to judge or condemn.
- *Impartiality*. Impartial people are unbiased and unwavering. They don't compromise the truth in a difficult situation. Wise people are steady.
- *Sincerity*. A wise mom doesn't say she believes one thing, then act out something else. Sincerity leaves no room for hypocrisy.

It would be as impossible to cultivate these qualities by ourselves as it would be to grow a garden without seeds. But when we have been cleansed by Christ's blood and we remain close to him, we—and our children—will see that these fruits grow in our lives.

> God of wisdom,
> Thank you that as we walk near you, we will grow in purity, peace, consideration, submission, mercy, impartiality, and sincerity. Amen.

*O*ver the years I've prayed that my sons would grow in their love for God and his Word, but sometimes I forget that it's often the challenges of life that send us running there.

I'll never forget the afternoon I picked up one of my sons from high school and could tell by the way he walked to the car that he'd had a dismal day. After he told me about a big disappointment (his girlfriend had informed friends at school that she was breaking up with him before she told him), I redirected our van to Taco Bell. As the mother of boys, I've discovered that a favorite snack often helps promote good conversation. When we returned home and sat at the kitchen table, I listened to his feelings and tried to encourage him the best I could.

Later that afternoon, I walked upstairs to check on my son in his bedroom, and I noticed that his eyes were red. As I sat down next to him, I noticed something else. On his desk was his open Bible. When I asked him what he was reading, he said, "Hebrews 13:5, where God promises that he will never leave us or forsake us." Then it was my turn to get misty eyes.

That experience reminded me why it's important to saturate a child's life with reverent knowledge of God's Word. Then, when they need hope, they know exactly where to turn. Ruth Graham wisely wrote: "If our children have the background of . . . unshakable faith that the Bible is indeed the Word of God, they will have a foundation that the forces of hell cannot shake."

Father,
Help us to cherish the Bible so that our children will cherish it, too.
Thanks for the encouragement your Word brings to people of all ages.
In Jesus' name, amen.

GIVE THANKS TO THE LORD, FOR HE IS GOOD! HIS
FAITHFUL LOVE ENDURES FOREVER. HAS THE LORD
REDEEMED YOU? THEN SPEAK OUT! TELL OTHERS HE HAS SAVED
YOU FROM YOUR ENEMIES.

Psalm 107:1-2

*Y*oung children often get their words mixed up. My kids used to say *hangaburger* instead of hamburger and *skabetti* instead of spaghetti. Perhaps one of the more memorable word slips for our two-year-old son, Chad, was his version of a children's praise song. Instead of "Praise him, Praise him, all ye little children," he sang "Praise him, Praise him, *naughty* little children." When one of our friends from church heard Chad singing the incorrect—albeit cute—version of the song, he remarked, "Well, he does have his theology straight."

Only in heaven does God hear perfect praise. This side of heaven, there's just no such thing. If we waited until we were "good enough," praise would never happen. But isn't that the point? Isn't that exactly why we praise him? None of us *are* good enough! We praise God because of what he has done in sending Jesus to die on the cross for our sins and provide forgiveness, healing, and hope for us all.

Seeing God take care of me and provide for me in the middle of my neediness is one thing that prompts me to praise him. In fact, I've noticed that great trials often prompt great praise. When I see how strong and righteous God is compared to how weak and needy I am, it's hard to keep that kind of good news to myself.

Father,
Thank you that you love us so much that you want to hear our imperfect
praises. May we be willing to speak out and tell others what you have done for
us. In Jesus' name, amen.

SERVICE

AND THEN HE TOLD THEM, "GO INTO ALL THE WORLD
AND PREACH THE GOOD NEWS TO EVERYONE, EVERYWHERE."

Mark 16:15

We can teach our children nothing more important than the gospel of Jesus Christ, because it has eternal implications for their souls. The good news about Jesus was prophesied in the Old Testament: Jesus was born as a man into King David's royal family line, he lived on earth for a while, he died a terrible death on a cross, and he was proven to be the Son of God when God raised him from the dead through the power of the Holy Spirit. God did all this to save us from the penalty of our sin, so that we could believe him, obey him, and bring glory to him (Romans 1:3-5).

I'm sometimes hesitant to share God's Good News for fear that I won't deliver it perfectly or that it won't be received perfectly. But perhaps a better way to look at it is this: If my children (or neighbors, relatives, or friends) were in a burning building and there was plenty of time for me to warn them to get out, would I wait until I could say, "Get out of the building and go to a safe place" with perfect tact? Of course not! I'd deliver the message because it was urgent and because—if they acted on it—it would save their lives. So does the Good News of Jesus Christ.

When we share the good news with our children or friends or relatives, we tell them what Christ has done for us. As others have said, it's as though each of us is one beggar telling another beggar where she found bread.

Father,
Thank you that the good news of Jesus gives us purpose now and hope for the future. Please help us to serve you by spreading the good news, beginning in our homes. Amen.

WORK

FOR WE ARE GOD'S MASTERPIECE. HE HAS CREATED US
ANEW IN CHRIST JESUS, SO THAT WE CAN DO THE GOOD
THINGS HE PLANNED FOR US LONG AGO.   *Ephesians 2:10*

Work. To some the word sounds depressing. To others it sounds energizing. I believe that our perspective on life and eternity helps determine our attitude toward work.

While on an airplane flight, I picked up the March 1998 copy of *Hemisphere* magazine and read an article about Millard Fuller, the founder of Habitat for Humanity. At age twenty-nine, Fuller became a millionaire while working as a lawyer and was living with a pretty fancy roof over his head. But after a marital crisis, he and his wife decided to downscale and seek a path of service. They searched for a way to make their lives count for God's work in the world.

Discovering that one great need in our nation was housing for low-income families, they began a program of building houses for the poor. Fuller stated that the majority of volunteers who work with Habitat do so because of religious motivation. He calls it the "theology of the hammer." Putting their faith into action, people use hammers as tools that demonstrate love.

As a mother, I don't have to search very far before I find ways that my life can count for God's work in the world. I prepare meals and pray that God's Word will nourish my children's souls. I do laundry and pray for the purity of my children. I encourage Christian character in them, praying that God will use them to build Christian families. The important thing is that all our work is done with a goal of furthering God's Kingdom.

God,
Thank you for examples of people who want their lives to count for you. May our lives count for you as we serve you inside and outside our homes. Amen.

WORK

THE CROWD WAS LISTENING TO EVERYTHING JESUS SAID.
AND BECAUSE HE WAS NEARING JERUSALEM, HE TOLD A STORY
TO CORRECT THE IMPRESSION THAT THE KINGDOM OF GOD WOULD
BEGIN RIGHT AWAY. HE SAID, "A NOBLEMAN WAS CALLED AWAY TO A DISTANT
EMPIRE TO BE CROWNED KING AND THEN RETURN. BEFORE HE LEFT, HE CALLED
TOGETHER TEN SERVANTS AND GAVE THEM TEN POUNDS OF SILVER TO INVEST FOR
HIM WHILE HE WAS GONE."

Luke 19:11-13

*S*omething new jumped out at me when I read Jesus' parable of the king's servants today. I knew that the parable focused on three servants who had been given money to invest. What I forgot was that money had been given to *ten* servants—not just three. Surprisingly, we never find out what happened to the other seven.

In the parable, a nobleman informed ten servants that he was going away to be crowned king, but that he would return. Before he left, he gave each of the servants some money to invest while he was gone. When the king returned, he summoned the servants and asked what they had done with his money. The parable recounts that the first two who reported to him had invested the money and gained a profit, but the third had kept it in secret because of his fear.

The whole point of investing is that we contribute money to make more money. The *Dean Witter Guide to Personal Investing* reports that if a thirty-year-old begins investing $150 a month at 10 percent interest, by the time he or she is sixty-five, the investment will have grown to about $574,000. Sounds good!

As a follower of Christ, I too have been given resources to help build and expand God's Kingdom. God has blessed me with life, breath, energy, time, children, his Word, his church, his Spirit, gifts, meaningful work, and an income. How am I managing those gifts? How am I contributing to those gifts? What kind of return is God getting on his investment in me?

Father,
We want to be faithful servants. Please help us to manage your resources well.
In Jesus' name, amen.

SALVATION

FOR THE GRACE OF GOD HAS BEEN REVEALED, BRINGING
SALVATION TO ALL PEOPLE.   *Titus 2:11*

*D*uring the summer, my sons and I used to spend time at our community's swimming pool whenever the weather allowed. I was impressed with the many lifeguards stationed every few feet around the pool. Usually they were a quiet presence, but one day my youngest son and I saw a lifeguard perform the service she was trained to do—deliver a swimmer from difficulty and drowning.

A little girl around the age of five had jumped off the highest diving board. After entering the water, she surfaced but was thrashing and gasping for air, unable to swim from the middle of the pool over to the edge. The lifeguard blew her whistle, promptly jumped in, rescued the little girl, and delivered her to the edge of the pool. Once the child was out of the water, she was visibly upset but all right. Everyone nearby heaved a sigh of relief!

My son had heard the word *salvation* many times, but that day he had a mental picture of it—deliverance from difficulty or death. Just as every swimmer in the pool was within sight of a lifeguard, so every person in the world is within sight of God. Salvation through Jesus has appeared to *all*, and all of us need to realize that we cannot make it through life on our own. The Bible teaches that for us to experience salvation, we need to believe that Jesus is God and turn to him in saving faith.

Through a common experience of going to the pool, we witnessed a not-so-common rescue. It was a reminder to me and to my son that God's plan for the whole world is salvation.

God,
We're thankful whenever a person is rescued from difficulty or distress. Thank
you that because of your death on the cross, you have offered us salvation.
Amen.

SALVATION

FOR GOD IN ALL HIS FULLNESS WAS PLEASED TO LIVE IN
CHRIST, AND BY HIM GOD RECONCILED EVERYTHING TO HIMSELF.
HE MADE PEACE WITH EVERYTHING IN HEAVEN AND ON EARTH BY MEANS
OF HIS BLOOD ON THE CROSS.

Colossians 1:19-20

I reserve one small drawer in my dresser for papers and notes that hold special meaning to me. Recently I noticed that the drawer was getting a little messy, so I decided to sort through the contents, getting rid of whatever I could and tidying the rest.

As you might imagine, I got caught up in reading the notes and appreciating the memories. One item that I'll never part with was given to me by my oldest son, Chad, when he was six. It consists of several small pieces of notebook paper that Chad cut, fashioned, and taped into the shape of a cross. On the cross, Chad drew a stick figure picture of Jesus, with nails through his hands and feet—and a smile on his face.

"The cross," says Dietrich Bonhoeffer, "is God's truth about us, and therefore it is the only power which can make us truthful. When we know the cross, we are no longer afraid of the truth." Embracing the truth of the cross has made a difference in Chad's priorities. Because of the cross, Chad finds service to Christ more important than money, power, or pleasure. Because of the cross, Chad cares about other people's hearts. I'm grateful the cross of Christ had an impact on Chad's young heart at the age of six and that it continues to have an impact on him today at twenty-six.

> *Father,*
> *Thank you that we can have peace with you because of Jesus' death on the cross. Thank you that the truth of the cross is life changing. In the precious name of Jesus, amen.*

WORK

I HAVE BROUGHT YOU GLORY ON EARTH BY
COMPLETING THE WORK YOU GAVE ME TO DO.   *John 17:4, NIV*

*N*one of us is perfect, and no mom on earth will ever do a perfect job of mothering. But when you come to the end of your mothering days, will you feel that you have completed your tasks well? When Jesus was nearing the end of his time on earth, he didn't have regrets; rather, he spoke with confidence about completing God's work. What was God's work for Jesus, and how can we be sure that *we* are completing God's work in our mothering?

Jesus gave us a lifelong pattern to follow:

1. *He pointed people to God.* John 1:18 says, "No one has ever seen God. But his only Son, who is himself God, is near to the Father's heart; he has told us about him."

2. *He modeled justice, mercy, and humility.* Micah 6:8 states, "No, O people, the Lord has already told you what is good, and this is what he requires: to do what is right, to love mercy, and to walk humbly with your God."

3. *He made disciples.* He said, "Therefore, go and make disciples of all the nations, baptizing them in the name of the Father and the Son and the Holy Spirit. Teach these new disciples to obey all the commands I have given you. And be sure of this: I am with you always, even to the end of the age" (Matthew 28:19-20).

4. *He served through sacrifice.* Philippians 2:5-8 says, "Your attitude should be the same that Christ Jesus had. Though he was God, he did not demand and cling to his rights as God. He made himself nothing; he took the humble position of a slave and appeared in human form. And in human form he obediently humbled himself even further by dying a criminal's death on a cross."

God,
Thank you that Jesus was willing to do your work so we can have a relationship with you. Please strengthen us to do the most important work of motherhood by pointing our children to you; modeling mercy, justice, and humility; discipling our kids; and serving through sacrifice. Amen.

CHRIST'S PASSION

AND SO, DEAR BROTHERS AND SISTERS, WE CAN BOLDLY
ENTER HEAVEN'S MOST HOLY PLACE BECAUSE OF THE BLOOD
OF JESUS. THIS IS THE NEW, LIFE-GIVING WAY THAT CHRIST HAS OPENED
UP FOR US THROUGH THE SACRED CURTAIN, BY MEANS OF HIS DEATH FOR US. AND
SINCE WE HAVE A GREAT HIGH PRIEST WHO RULES OVER GOD'S PEOPLE, LET US GO
RIGHT INTO THE PRESENCE OF GOD, WITH TRUE HEARTS FULLY TRUSTING HIM.
FOR OUR EVIL CONSCIENCES HAVE BEEN SPRINKLED WITH CHRIST'S BLOOD TO
MAKE US CLEAN, AND OUR BODIES HAVE BEEN WASHED WITH PURE WATER.

Hebrews 10:19-22

What kind of window coverings do you use in your home? My favorites are the floral valances hanging in my living room. When my family first moved into our home, the valances helped pull all of our colors together. And when we repainted our walls taupe, my neighbor suggested tea-staining the valances to get a new effect. It worked nicely, so the valances are still hanging.

During the time that Jesus was on earth, a heavy curtain hung in the Temple and separated the Holy Place (which only priests could enter) from the Most Holy Place (which only the high priest could enter, and then only once a year to make amends for the sins of the people). This curtain holds a significant place in the story of Jesus' crucifixion.

Matthew 27:50-53 explains that at the very moment Jesus died, while an earthquake opened some graves and saints rose from the dead, the curtain in the temple was torn from top to bottom! Only God could have done that. This Passion event holds great symbolism for us: Since that moment when the curtain was torn, the way to God has been opened. All of us may come to him.

The curtain is no longer necessary. There is no more need for temples, altars, or animal sacrifices, because Jesus—through his death for our sins—provided the way to God. This is huge! Any person who has trusted in Christ's death and resurrection can communicate directly with God—anytime and anywhere. Have you placed your faith in Christ's death for your sin on the cross? Are you enjoying the access Christ offers you to the presence of God?

Father,
Thank you for the image of a torn curtain, reminding us that if we place our faith in Jesus' death and resurrection, nothing holds us back from communicating directly with you. In Jesus' name, amen.

CHOICES

TODAY I HAVE GIVEN YOU THE CHOICE BETWEEN LIFE AND
DEATH, BETWEEN BLESSINGS AND CURSES. I CALL ON HEAVEN
AND EARTH TO WITNESS THE CHOICE YOU MAKE. OH, THAT YOU
WOULD CHOOSE LIFE, THAT YOU AND YOUR DESCENDANTS MIGHT LIVE!

Deuteronomy 30:19

To choose is to select from a number of possibilities, and we do it all day long. When my children come to the table for breakfast, will I set out cereal, or will I cook eggs? Will I walk today or not? Moving on to some bigger choices, will I send my children to private schools or public schools, or will I home school? Out of the many churches in my community, which body will I worship with?

If the breakfast issue is a "baby bear" choice, and the school and church issues are "mama bear" choices, I believe a "papa bear" choice is presented in Deuteronomy 30:19.

Moses explained to the children of Israel that they had a choice to make, and it was a choice to be made with their hearts. Moses asked the people to choose between life and death, blessings and curses. The question of the day was, "Do you choose God—yes or no?"

Paul presented that choice to his readers in Romans 10:6-10, and we have the same choice before us today. We can choose Christ and walk in his ways, or we can be drawn to other gods, bringing a curse upon ourselves. Simply stated, a choice for Christ brings life and blessing for us and for our children.

Giver of life,
Thank you that you didn't make us robots, but you created us with the ability
to choose. With the power of your Spirit, help us to make choices for you and
your Kingdom. Amen.

WITNESS

YOU ARE THE SALT OF THE EARTH. BUT WHAT GOOD IS
SALT IF IT HAS LOST ITS FLAVOR? CAN YOU MAKE IT USEFUL AGAIN?
IT WILL BE THROWN OUT AND TRAMPLED UNDERFOOT AS WORTHLESS.
YOU ARE THE LIGHT OF THE WORLD—LIKE A CITY ON A MOUNTAIN, GLOWING IN
THE NIGHT FOR ALL TO SEE. DON'T HIDE YOUR LIGHT UNDER A BASKET! INSTEAD,
PUT IT ON A STAND AND LET IT SHINE FOR ALL.   *Matthew 5:13-15*

While doing some last-minute shopping one week before Christmas, I stumbled on a sale at Gap. Several racks of young men's sweaters had been priced at ten dollars each—a big bargain for sweaters I knew my sons would enjoy.

After purchasing three sweaters, I left the store feeling excited about discovering such a great sale. Thinking that the news was too good to keep to myself, I mentioned it to several friends I spoke with throughout the day. If my friends still had any shopping left to do, I figured they might find something for their kids too.

Later, I got to thinking about my happy discovery and the excitement with which I shared it. Why is it, I thought, that I'll call a friend and share good news about a sale on sweaters at Gap, but sometimes I'm not as quick to share good news about gifts that Christ has given to me?

Through Christ's death and resurrection, I've received peace with God, a new identity, forgiveness of sin, the presence of God's Spirit, wisdom for the asking, and much more. I wouldn't call a friend and itemize every Christmas gift I'd bought, nor would I call a friend and describe everything Christ has done for me—the lists would be too long. But I can share *one* way that Christ is helping me today. I can witness about Christ's gifts—one person at a time.

Father,
Thank you for the privilege of representing you to others. Help us to do it
with joy. Amen.

If we set out to bake cupcakes with our children, we teach them to measure correctly. Why? The way we measure affects the outcome of the cake. God's Word teaches us that the way we measure our lives affects the outcome of our hearts. In the verse above, we're taught to number our days "aright." That word is significant. We all number our days (by years), but what does it mean to do it "aright"? The preceding verses in Psalm 90 help us see the plan:

1. Realize that God lives forever. History comes and history goes, but God is eternal, and he exists far above the events on earth. No matter what generation a person lives in, he always has the opportunity to choose God as his dwelling-place, his eternal refuge.

2. Realize that our earthly lives are temporary. In verses 3-6, our lives are likened to dust, a watch in the night (about three or four hours long), and grass that springs up in the morning but withers at night.

3. Realize that our life only counts for eternity if we choose to be in proper relationship with the God of eternity. Because God made us in his image, if we choose to honor him with our lives, they can mean something and accomplish something. Our brief lives on earth can help to further his kingdom—especially through lives of the children he has given us.

Using our time correctly *now* determines the outcome of our hearts *eternally*!

Father,
Psalm 90:12 is an appropriate prayer for us each day of our earthly existence:
"Teach us to number our days aright, that we may gain a heart of wisdom."
Thank you that even though we are frail humans, we can choose to be
connected to the eternal God through faith in Jesus Christ! Amen.

WE DON'T GO AROUND PREACHING ABOUT OURSELVES; WE
PREACH CHRIST JESUS, THE LORD. ALL WE SAY ABOUT OURSELVES
IS THAT WE ARE YOUR SERVANTS BECAUSE OF WHAT JESUS HAS DONE FOR
US. FOR GOD, WHO SAID, "LET THERE BE LIGHT IN THE DARKNESS," HAS MADE US
UNDERSTAND THAT THIS LIGHT IS THE BRIGHTNESS OF THE GLORY OF GOD THAT IS
SEEN IN THE FACE OF JESUS CHRIST.   *2 Corinthians 4:5-6*

After World War II, German students volunteered to help rebuild a cathedral in England, one of many casualties of the Luftwaffe bombings. As the work progressed, debate broke out on how to best restore a large statue of Jesus with His arms outstretched and bearing the familiar inscription, "Come unto Me." Careful patching could repair all damage to the statue except for Christ's hands, which had been destroyed by bomb fragments. Should they attempt the delicate task of reshaping those hands?

Finally the workers reached a decision that still stands today. The statue of Jesus had no hands, and the inscription now reads, "Christ has no hands but ours."4

Over the years, we use our hands to point out many things to our children. While reading a book to a toddler, we point to a cow, asking, "What's that?" While baking chocolate chip cookies with a daughter, we point to the recipe to determine how much sugar we need. While riding in the car with our student driver, we point to the upcoming exit ramp and suggest moving into the right lane.

Of all the things moms point their children to, nothing is as important to their well-being as pointing them to Christ. We point them to the Light of the World because we don't want them to stumble in the darkness. We point them to the Bread of Life because we don't want them to be spiritually hungry. We point them to the Savior because we don't want them to live as slaves to sin. Nothing compares with the privilege of pointing our children to Christ.

God,
Thank you that you sent us light when you sent Christ—and thank you that you allow us to be your hands in this world. Please equip us for the privilege we've been given of pointing our children to Christ. In Christ's name, amen.

WORK

MAY THE FAVOR OF THE LORD OUR GOD REST UPON
US; ESTABLISH THE WORK OF OUR HANDS FOR US—YES,
ESTABLISH THE WORK OF OUR HANDS.   *Psalm 90:17, NIV*

I was amazed at the amount of space the word *work* is given in the dictionary—one and a half columns! But then I got to thinking that a whole lot of my life is spent working—giving physical or mental effort toward the production or accomplishment of some task or goal. I have invested hours of work in my children's lives—nursing, feeding, holding, singing, dressing, reading, putting together puzzles, going to church, driving, hosting friends, cooking, praying, listening, talking, doing laundry, and providing music lessons. Those are all part of a mother's work. Is it producing or accomplishing something? You bet! What a joy for a mom to see her children growing, maturing, and accomplishing things on their own.

It's especially meaningful to think that my work has not only been aimed at the years of my children's life spans. Because I am in relationship with the eternal God, my work has been aimed toward eternity. When I look, with gratitude, at the choices my sons are making in their late teens and early twenties, I understand a little bit of what it means to see my work *established*, as mentioned in the above verse. To establish something is to make it firm and secure, to place or settle it in a secure position or condition. As moms, that is the goal of our work.

No matter what stage of motherhood we're at or how many mistakes we've made, we can pray that God will help us focus our work of motherhood on eternity.

Father,
May we realize that the work we do today has an impact on eternity. Amen.

HOPE

THIS IS WHAT THE LORD SAYS: "CURSED ARE THOSE WHO
PUT THEIR TRUST IN MERE HUMANS AND TURN THEIR HEARTS
AWAY FROM THE LORD. THEY ARE LIKE STUNTED SHRUBS IN THE DESERT,
WITH NO HOPE FOR THE FUTURE. THEY WILL LIVE IN THE BARREN WILDERNESS,
ON THE SALTY FLATS WHERE NO ONE LIVES. BUT BLESSED ARE THOSE WHO TRUST IN
THE LORD AND HAVE MADE THE LORD THEIR HOPE AND CONFIDENCE. THEY ARE
LIKE TREES PLANTED ALONG A RIVERBANK, WITH ROOTS THAT REACH DEEP INTO
THE WATER. SUCH TREES ARE NOT BOTHERED BY THE HEAT OR WORRIED BY LONG
MONTHS OF DROUGHT. THEIR LEAVES STAY GREEN, AND THEY GO RIGHT ON
PRODUCING DELICIOUS FRUIT."

Jeremiah 17:5-8

If I was thinking of launching a landscaping company and I asked my children whether I should locate it in the desert or next to a riverbank, they would say, "Well, that's a no-brainer!" The first location would spell doom; the second would predict success. Each of us has a similar choice about where we will locate the landscape of our life. Will we place our hope in mere humans, or will we place it in the Lord? The way we live out the answer to that question concludes whether our hearts will be empty or full.

"Where do you want to place your hope?" Jeremiah asks us. "In a fallible person who might live for about eighty years, or in the all-powerful Creator who lives forever?" How we answer his question determines whether we will look like a measly, undersized bush or a flourishing plant. It determines whether we will live a life that's unproductive or a life that's abundant. Do we want to be depleted and empty, or do we want to be full? I vote for full.

Father,
Thanks for vivid descriptions of things like shrubs, trees, deserts, and river-
banks that remind us to put our trust in you. Amen.

LOVE

MAY YOUR ROOTS GO DOWN DEEP INTO THE SOIL OF
GOD'S MARVELOUS LOVE. AND MAY YOU HAVE THE POWER TO
UNDER-STAND, AS ALL GOD'S PEOPLE SHOULD, HOW WIDE, HOW
LONG, HOW HIGH, AND HOW DEEP HIS LOVE REALLY IS. MAY YOU EXPERIENCE THE
LOVE OF CHRIST, THOUGH IT IS SO GREAT YOU WILL NEVER FULLY UNDERSTAND
IT. THEN YOU WILL BE FILLED WITH THE FULLNESS OF LIFE AND POWER THAT
COMES FROM GOD.   *Ephesians 3:17-19*

*S*ome time ago my husband and a friend had breakfast together. His friend
posed the question, "When we get to heaven, what do you think is going to be the
biggest surprise of all?" After thinking it over, my husband replied, "I think we'll
be surprised by the overwhelming depth of God's love for us."

In today's passage, Paul's prayer for the Ephesians explores the scope of
God's love—how wide, how long, how high, and how deep it is. Paul wants us
not only to have an intellectual understanding of the love of Christ but also to experience that love. He tells us that Christ's love is so great that we will never fully
understand it! Thankfully, we can experience it even without understanding it.

The shore of a great ocean is one of the best places to think about the extremes
of God's love. As far as our eyes can see to the left, to the right, and straight
across, there is no end in sight. What a wonderful picture of the extent of God's
love.

A songwriter puts it this way:

> *Could we with ink the ocean fill*
> *And were the skies of parchment made,*
> *Were every stalk on earth a quill*
> *And every man a scribe by trade,*
> *To write the love of God above*
> *Would drain the ocean dry,*
> *Nor could the scroll contain the whole*
> *Tho' stretched from sky to sky.*[15]

Father,
Please fill us with your love that is deep and wide so that we will live a full
life for you. In Jesus' name, amen.

HEAVEN

Last summer I spent a weekend visiting with my two sisters, Gail and Barbara. The three of us stayed at a hotel in Cedar Rapids, Iowa, and enjoyed a few days of walking, talking, shopping, and playing games.

The first morning we walked, we explored a neighborhood near the hotel. To our pleasant surprise, we stumbled on Noel Ridge, a sprawling park that contained acres of gorgeous flowers and groundcovers. It was a gardener's delight. The three of us walked from one tier of gardens to another, stopping to admire the beauty and variety of each section. Although I'm not the gardener that either of my sisters is, I came away with a few new planting ideas for next year: "Forever Blue" eustoma, "Lavender Lace" cuphea, and pink alteranthera. I don't know how to *pronounce* any of those names, much less grow them, but it will be fun to give them a try.

As I wandered around the colorful gardens, the words of a song came to mind:

> *Heav'n above is softer blue,*
> *Earth around is sweeter green!*
> *Something lives in ev'ry hue*
> *Christless eyes have never seen:*
> *Birds with gladder song o'erflow*
> *Flow'rs with deeper beauties shine,*
> *Since I know, as now I know,*
> *I am His and He is mine.*[16]

While living on this earth, I have opportunities to appreciate a tiny percentage of the wonders and works of our Creator. But I hope that when I get to heaven, I'll be able to admire every single flower and plant that God created. I can't imagine what it will be like to stroll through *that* garden.

> *Father in heaven,*
> *Thanks for little tastes of heaven that you give us here on earth. Amen.*

CHRISTMAS

NOW THERE WAS A MAN NAMED SIMEON WHO LIVED IN
JERUSALEM. HE WAS A RIGHTEOUS MAN AND VERY DEVOUT.
HE WAS FILLED WITH THE HOLY SPIRIT, AND HE EAGERLY
EXPECTED THE MESSIAH TO COME AND RESCUE ISRAEL. THE HOLY SPIRIT HAD
REVEALED TO HIM THAT HE WOULD NOT DIE UNTIL HE HAD SEEN THE LORD'S
MESSIAH. THAT DAY THE SPIRIT LED HIM TO THE TEMPLE. SO WHEN MARY AND
JOSEPH CAME TO PRESENT THE BABY JESUS TO THE LORD AS THE LAW REQUIRED,
SIMEON WAS THERE.

Luke 2:25-28

I've always been intrigued by the Bible's accounts of lesser-known characters surrounding the birth of Christ. One of those characters was an old man named Simeon, and there's a lot of wonder packed into the ten short verses that tell his story.

Simeon was a Jew who lived in Jerusalem at the time Jesus was born. The words used to describe him—righteous and devout—are very telling. They inform us that Simeon was upright, godly, sincere, earnest, and passionate in his beliefs. The Bible goes on to tell us that God's spirit not only filled Simeon's life but had also revealed to Simeon that he would not die until he had seen the Messiah.

Eight days after Jesus was born, Mary and Joseph fulfilled the law of Moses by taking Jesus to the Temple, presenting him to the Lord. That very day, God's spirit led Simeon to the Temple, and he had a part in the ceremony! As Simeon took Jesus into his arms, he praised God, saying, "Lord, now I can die in peace! As you promised me, I have seen the Savior you have given to all people. He is a light to reveal God to the nations, and he is the glory of your people Israel!" (Luke 2:29-32).

What an example of faith Simeon is for us. He was eager for Jesus to bring light to all peoples, and as a result of his righteous and devout life he was ready to be used at just the right time for God's divine purposes. May we be every bit as eager to see the light of Jesus shine in our lives and families.

Father,
Thank you for the way you arrange for people like Simeon to be in just the right place at just the right time. We ask for your help as we cooperate with you to bring the Good News of Jesus to others. In the name of Jesus, our Savior, amen.

NOTES

[1] Bruce B. Barton, et al., *Life Application Bible Commentary, John* (Wheaton, Ill.: Tyndale House, 1993), 276.

[2] James S. Hewett, *Illustrations Unlimited* (Wheaton, Ill.: Tyndale House, 1989), 380.

[3] Philip Yancey and Tim Stafford, *Unhappy Secrets of the Christian Life* (Grand Rapids, Mich./Wheaton, Ill.: Zondervan/Campus Life Books, 1979), 75.

[4] Phillips Brooks, "O Little Town of Bethlehem," copyright 1867.

[5] William Williams, "Guide Me, O Thou Great Jehovah," copyright 1745.

[6] Julia A. Fletcher, "Little Things," copyright 1845.

[7] Gary Smalley and John Trent, *The Blessing* (Nashville: Thomas Nelson, 1986), 81–82.

[8] Dr. Paul Brand and Philip Yancey, *Fearfully and Wonderfully Made* (Grand Rapids, Mich.: Zondervan, 1980), 195.

[9] Michael Horton, *We Believe* (Nashville: Word, 1998), 26–27.

[10] Ingrid Trobisch, *The Confident Woman* (New York: HarperCollins, 1993), 63.

[11] Robert Manson Myers, *Handel's Messiah, A Touchstone of Taste* (New York: Octagon Books, 1971), 63.

[12] R. Kent Hughes, *1,001 Great Stories & Quotes* (Wheaton, Ill.: Tyndale House, 1998), 135.

[13] Frances Ridley Havergal, "Like a River Glorious," copyright 1876.

[14] Keller, *A Shepherd Looks at Psalm 23,* 30.

[15] Frederick M. Lehman, "The Love of God," copyright 1917, renewed 1945 by Nazarene Publishing House. Used by permission.

[16] George Wade Robinson, "I Am His, and He Is Mine," copyright 1876.